LORI

I Love You, but...

GARY DAVIS

Covenant
Communications, Inc.

Revised and enlarged from a
story entitled *What Now, McBride?*

Covenant Communications, Inc.
American Fork, Utah

Printed in the United States of America
First Printing: August 1993
94 95 96 97   10 9 8 7 6 5 4 3 2

Lori, I Love You, But
ISBN 1-55503-579-5
Library of Congress Catalog Card Number: 93-79543

Covenant
Communications, Inc.

For
Doug
Steve
Shelann
and
Mike

• ONE •

"Weird-ville, dead ahead." Lori announced to herself upon spying the sign which read, Mormon Temple—Visitors Center. She wheeled her red Miata off Santa Monica Boulevard, up a short hill, and into the parking lot adjacent to the Los Angeles Temple. Lori sat for some moments looking at the large, stately structure with the gold-plated statue atop its single spire. Several acres of immaculately landscaped grounds surrounded the building.

"Not exactly Temple Beth El," she mused, thinking of the small Jewish synagogue she attended as a child.

Referring to Mormons as "weird" was nothing personal, Lori Klein considered all religion to be superstitious mumbo-jumbo and its adherents to be a few slices short of a full pizza. She was, after all, an enlightened woman of the nineties, a mature, sophisticated, nearly twenty-year-old, college sophomore.

Lori was also a procrastinator, which was why she was at the Mormon Temple that particular day. She had an eight-page report due for a philosophy class in just two days. The subject was religion, and Lori was growing desperate. Had she started sooner, Lori would have chosen one of the more exotic sounding groups, like the Moonies or Hare Krishna. In addition, half a dozen "New Age" religions also flourished in the area and might have caught her attention. At this point though, time was running out. So when she heard there was a Mormon, "Visitors' Center," just a few miles from the UCLA campus, it seemed like the answer to an atheist's prayer.

• *TWO* •

Returning to his car after attending a session at the temple, Jared noticed the slender brunette in the blue jeans and a loose, long-sleeved blouse standing on the steps outside the Visitors' Center. *Looks like a refugee from Philosophy 111*, Jared thought to himself. Remembering his boy scout training, he walked over to see if he could be of some assistance.

"Hi, would you like to take a tour?" he asked, flashing his finest smile.

Lori eyed the tall, blond young man suspiciously.

"How much does it cost?" She asked.

The question amused him. "That all depends on whether you want the mini, the regular, or the grand-spectacular tour."

"What's the difference?"

"Well, with the grand-spectacular we fly you in a private jet to Salt Lake City and introduce you personally to the Angel Moroni."

"Who?"

"Then it's off to the Holy Land, where you get to wail on the wailing wall and . . ."

"Listen, creep," She interrupted, "I'm just here to get some information for a philosophy report."

"Oh, in that case you probably want the regular tour," Jared said. "Just go in and join the group by the door.

Everything's free."

As Lori entered, a short, wiry man in his sixties was explaining the origin of the large white statue of Christ in the center of the room. A Japanese tourist, armed with three cameras, maneuvered to capture the best angle on his Minolta. The tour continued, and Lori heard a strange story about a farm boy, an angel, and some gold plates that were translated "by the gift and power of God." She smiled to herself, thinking how gullible the religious were. At the same time, she was surprised to learn that the guide, whose name tag showed him to be "Brother Sant," was a retired doctor who, along with his wife, was serving a mission for their church. *He's probably too cheap to play golf*, she thought. But he was a pleasant man who possessed an encyclopedic knowledge of his faith, which for the sake of her paper she was glad he had.

At the conclusion of the tour, a movie was shown. When the lights came on and the screen receded into the ceiling, the guide asked his audience for questions. Lori wanted to ask, "Do you really believe that junk?" but she didn't. No queries were forthcoming, so the good doctor decided to answer some that hadn't been asked, showing that he still had some unused information in reserve.

Before leaving, Lori bought an inexpensive copy of *The Book of Mormon*, signed the guest book, and gathered a handful of pamphlets.

• *THREE* •

Following his brief encounter with Lori Klein, Jared went to bid on a remodeling job not far from the Temple. The potential customer wasn't home, however, so he returned to the Visitors' Center thinking that perhaps he might find some company for lunch.

On the steps outside the Visitors' Center, Lori again encountered the young man with the infectious smile. "Hello again," he said "What did you think of the tour?"

"I thought it was a bunch of baloney," she replied bluntly.

Lori felt a nice glow of satisfaction seeing his silly grin fade to a look of pained dismay.

He leaned forward and lightly touched her arm.

"Tell me the truth," he said earnestly. "Are you just saying that to make me feel good?"

For a moment neither moved. Then the corners of his mouth began to curl, and in spite of herself, Lori smiled. Suddenly both of them were laughing. He extended his hand.

"I'm Jared Taylor."

"Jared," she repeated, sampling the name as though trying out a new flavor of ice cream.

"Of course some people call me 'creep,' but I prefer Jared."

They laughed again, and Lori looked a little embarrassed.

"I'm hungry. Are you?" Jared asked.

Lori didn't answer.

"Do you like Italian food?" Jared tried again.

"Depends." She said.

"On the company? Good! Come with me."

Jared took her arm, and they started toward the parking lot.

Lori pulled away. "You're insane! Where are we going?"

"Pasquales."

"Pasquales? Never heard of it."

"Pasquales has never heard of Lori Klein either," Jared told her matter of factly.

"How do you know my name?"

"I looked at the guest book."

"You're something else. Do you hang around here all the time trying to pick up girls?"

"No. Usually I hang around bars."

Lori stopped and faced him. "You're probably some kind of pervert."

Jared thought on that for a moment.

"Probably, but which kind?"

Lori laughed, and Jared joined her.

"Usually I can't stand someone who laughs at his own jokes," Lori informed him.

"Are you going to make an exception in my case?"

"No."

Jared smiled broadly.

"Good! I wouldn't want you patronizing me just because I'm a Mormon."

As they drove, Jared asked, "You're a student at UCLA?"

"Uh-huh."

"How do you like it?"

"It's okay. I just started there."

"You're from New York?"

"How'd you know?"

"Well, that's not exactly a Southern accent."

"What are you? A detective?"

He smiled. "I'm a building contractor."

"What kind of stuff do you build?"

"Houses mostly. Room additions, stuff like that."

"Do you like being a builder?"

"Most of the time."

Jared parked his orange VW Bug in front of a small restaurant sandwiched between a laundromat and a real estate office. "Here we are. The world-renowned Pasquales."

"It certainly looks impressive," Lori remarked dryly.

"Wait 'til you see the inside. It's still got Christmas decorations that were put up in 1974 and pictures of Italy with little sparkling lights in them. My personal favorite, of course, is a picture of a bunch of dogs sitting around a table playing poker."

"You really know how to impress a girl."

"It's nothing."

Lori rolled her eyes. "I believe that!"

Inside, half a dozen booths lined one wall, and several tables were randomly scattered about the dining area. The rear booth was stacked almost ceiling-high with empty pizza boxes. Only a few students and businessmen occupied the room.

Jared led Lori toward the booth nearest the pizza boxes. A balding, heavy-set man wearing a T-shirt and a food-stained apron peered out the kitchen door.

"Jimmy!" he called.

"Hey, Carmine! How'sa by you?" Jared yelled cheerfully.

"Sit down. I be right out."

"I thought your name was Jared," Lori asked as they settled into the booth.

"It is."

"Then why did he call you Jimmy?"

"Because I remind him of his nephew."

Lori smiled as she picked up a menu and asked, "What's good?"

"Well, they have terrific deep-dish pizza and the best

spaghetti on the block."

"How about the wine?"

"Wine? You're a wine buff? Miss Klein, this is your lucky day."

Just then the greasy apron appeared.

"Carmine, this young lady is a wine connoisseur. Please bring her a glass of your finest."

"Sure."

As the man disappeared back into the kitchen, and Lori cocked her head to one side and gave Jared the same look he had received when he asked if she wanted to tour the Visitor's Center.

"What are you smirking about?" she asked.

"Who's smirking?"

"You are. What's wrong with the wine?"

"You're a very suspicious person."

"I'm only suspicious of Mormons."

"How many Mormons do you know?"

"You're the first."

Jared chuckled and said, "I don't know anything about the wine here, except that Carmine makes his own, and he's very proud of it. I understand that he's done a good deal for temperance in the area, though."

The proprietor returned, handed Lori a cup of brown liquid, and stood back to await her appraisal.

"Now please note, Miss Klein, the delicate bouquet," Jared said in mock solemnity. "Notice also the container. This wine is much too fine to be served in an ordinary glass. No, indeed, only the finest imported styrofoam cups will do."

"Hey, Mormon, shut up!" Carmine interjected.

"You a Mormon?" he asked Lori.

"No."

"I didn't think so. Mormons don't drink. J'know that?"

Lori shook her head.

"They're culturally retarded," Carmine concluded.

"Hey, give us a break, Carmine. We started late. It takes

time to turn eight million people into winos."

Carmine ignored Jared's cheerful banter and returned his attention to Lori who was apprehensively eyeing her cup.

"What kind of wine is this?" she asked, stalling for time.

"It's white wine," Carmine announced proudly. "A Chablis."

"How come it's brown then?" Jared inquired.

"That's from the barrels," he answered defensively. "Lots of people use cheap barrels. I buy good barrels."

Lori took a sip and smiled weakly.

"Well, what do you think?" Carmine asked. "You can't buy wine like that in a store."

"No, no, it doesn't taste like store-bought wine," she agreed, blinking back tears.

"That's twenty-two percent alcohol," Carmine boasted.

"I think you've made a convert," Jared said. "Bring us five gallons."

"You're crazy, Jimmy."

"Thank you. I'd also like some pizza." Jared said. Turning to Lori, he asked, "Did you want something to eat, Miss, or were you planning to just sit and drink all afternoon?"

"Pizza sounds fine."

"Good."

"Bring us a medium combination and two dinner salads." Jared looked at Lori, and she nodded approval.

"You want everything on the pizza?" Carmine asked.

"Hold the anchovies and cockroaches," Jared ordered.

Carmine shook his head and mumbled a mild obscenity about Jared as he turned away.

"You're certainly a popular fellow here," Lori remarked.

"It's a gift."

"How lucky for you." She turned serious for a moment. "Could I ask you a personal question?"

"Sure."

"Do you believe that stuff about Smith and the angel?"

"Yes."

"That's incredible."

He smiled. "Is it more incredible than God parting the Red Sea for Moses?"

"No, but I don't believe that either."

"That's extremely serious, Klein."

Lori was pleased that he called her "Klein," although she didn't know why.

"What's the matter, you never met an atheist before?" Lori asked.

"You're an atheist?"

She nodded. "What of it?"

"Are you a devout atheist?"

"A what?"

"Well, a lot of people claim to be atheists, but as soon as things start going bad for them, they get religion. Very few atheists have the courage to stick to their lack of convictions. They're going around finding religion right and left and writing books about it. Gives the good atheists a bad name."

Lori eyed him pensively for a moment.

"Some day," she said, "they're going to put you in a home for unwed lunatics."

Jared smiled and said, "I like you, Klein."

"Are you just saying that to make me feel good?"

"Yes."

"Well, it doesn't."

"Sure it does."

Carmine returned with the salads. When he left, Jared leaned across the table. "Did you notice his apron?" he whispered.

"I smelled it," she answered.

"Every six months, he takes off his old apron, cuts it up in little squares, and serves it on a large pizza. It's terrific!"

Lori shook her head, then dug into her salad.

"What does your father do?" Jared asked.

"He owns a manufacturing plant."

"What do they make?"

"Shopping carts, mostly."

"Really? The kind with bad wheels that always pull to one side?"

Lori nodded. "You got it."

"Do you have any siblings?"

"One brother. He works for a computer outfit back in Connecticut. How about you?"

"Four sisters and one brother," Jared replied.

"What a tribe! Where do you fit in?"

"Number four. I have three married sisters, all older, and one sister who's a missionary in Mexico. My younger brother is with my folks in Australia."

"What are they doing in Australia?" Lori asked.

"Dad's a mission president for the Church. He's responsible for a couple hundred missionaries in the southeast part of Australia. They'll be gone two more years. Then they'll come home, and Dad will go back to his dental practice."

"He's a dentist?"

"Uh-huh. A mission president usually serves for three years and then goes back to whatever he was doing before."

"You mean the Church asks men to quit their jobs, pack up their families, and go halfway around the world?"

"Sometimes."

"What if they don't want to go?" Lori asked.

"They're taken out and shot."

"Seriously, what would happen?"

"Nothing. No one has to do anything in the Church."

"Would you go?"

"I already have."

"Where?"

"I spent two years as a missionary in Minnesota."

"Do a lot of Mormons do that?"

"Nearly fifty thousand are doing it right now. Most of them are young men around twenty, but quite a few women and retired couples go on missions, too."

"What does a Mormon missionary do?"

Jared thought for a moment. "He tries to change the world."

"Did you succeed?"

"Didn't you notice?" Jared smiled.

"I guess I wasn't paying attention."

Lori waited for a moment but Jared said nothing. He was thinking of memorable times shared with special people during the two years he had spent as a full-time missionary. He rarely thought of the rejections, or the difficult or the monotonous times. He thought about love and brotherhood and changed lives.

Lori felt uneasy by the shift in mood.

Sensing that, Jared asked, "What are you majoring in at UCLA?"

"Theater Arts."

"You are! I had no idea I was in the presence of a starlet. Carmine! Another gallon of wine! Do you have any talent?"

"Of course."

"What have you done?"

"I played the lead in *Hello Dolly* at Syracuse last year, and I did *The Good-bye Girl* in high school and *Send Me No Flowers* this past summer in Community Theater."

"I'm impressed! Do you sing?"

"Of course. How else would I do *Hello Dolly*?"

"I thought maybe they just played Barbara Streisand, and you did lip sync."

"Very funny. Is this a job interview?"

"Could be. I have influence with some very important people in Hollywood."

"I'll bet!"

Jared smiled. "Actually, I do know someone who might be able to help you."

"Works in the mail room at Universal, I suppose."

"Psychologists tell us, Miss Klein, that cynical people are deeply disturbed. For your information, I have a brother-in-law who's a director."

"Do you really?"

"I really do."

"What's he directed?"

"Well, he did *The Good-bye Girl* at some schlock high school in New York, and he also . . ."

"You're sick! Do you know that?"

"I know I am. I need your help."

"You're beyond help."

"Be nice to me, or I won't buy you any more wine."

"Are you putting me on about your brother-in-law?"

"No. His name is David Jennings. He's done work on *Taxi* and *The Wonder Years*. He started out doing commercials. Right now he's back East shooting a feature."

"How could he help me?"

"I don't know for sure, but he's been around the industry for several years. He could probably tell you some short cuts, help you get your SAG card. Maybe arrange some interviews. Would you like to meet him?"

"Sure."

"Okay. I'll arrange it when he gets back in town. Do you have a bio?"

"No."

"Pictures?"

"No."

"If you're going to be a star, you've got to get organized. There's a photographer in Glendale, Bob Gann, on South Central. He'll do a good job on your pictures, and he won't rip you off. Tell him you know me. Can you type?"

"Yes."

"Better type something up lying about how great you are. You won't need it when you talk to Dave, but you will later."

"How do you know about all this stuff?"

"I've been around the business all my life. My mother was an actress before she and Dad got married, and she's worked as a writer for half a dozen shows. Two of my sisters have been involved in the industry, and my dad worked as a studio musician while he was in college. I've done some acting, too."

"In what?"

Jared leaned forward and assumed a confidential tone. "For out senior play. We did *Mr. Roberts,* and I was Ensign Pulver. I stole the show."

"So how come you pound nails for a living?"

"I like to eat regularly. But I plan to write."

"A writer? What are you going to write?"

"Ultimately, I want to do screenplays."

"Have you sold anything?"

"A few short stories and some script ideas. I'm just learning the craft. I'd like to build a couple of houses a year and write the rest of the time."

Carmine arrived with the pizza.

"Thank you, my good man," Jared said.

He and Lori grabbed a wedge, and Jared went on.

"Acting's too unstable. One year you're a star, and the next year you can't even get an audition. Only a few can stay near the top. It's a very fickle business. You'd be better off to major in accounting and go to work for your father in the shopping cart factory."

"Thanks, but I'll take my chances out here," Lori said.

"I thought so."

They finished lunch. Lori poured her wine in a bed of artificial flowers behind the booth, and they walked to the counter at the rear where Jared paid the bill.

"Hey, Carmine, are you going to be open on Thanksgiving?" Jared asked.

"Why? You wanna buy a turkey pizza?" Carmine laughed uproariously.

"No, of course not. I need some spaghetti."

"Spaghetti?"

"Yeah, my grandmother has this fantastic recipe for stuffing that uses spaghetti. Haven't you heard of that?"

"No, I never heard of it."

"Really? That surprises me. How much spaghetti do you

think it would take to stuff a two hundred pound bird?"

"Two hundred pounds! You crazy?! Ain't no turkey in the world weighs two hundred pounds!" Carmine protested.

"Well, I know that, Carmine. I'm not that stupid. These are specially bred birds from South Dakota, not turkeys."

"Yeah, well, I know it couldn't be no turkey," he said, lowering his voice several decibels. "Two hundred pounds, no way."

"No, of course not. That would be ridiculous," Jared agreed.

"What kinda bird is it?"

"Excuse me?" Jared said, pretending not to hear.

"I said what kinda bird is it?"

Jared leaned slightly across the counter and waited for Carmine's full attention.

"Humming," he replied.

• *FOUR* •

Lori felt good as she drove back to campus. She had returned from her journey into the mysterious Mormon unknown both unbloody and unbowed. She had been neither intimidated nor embarrassed. She'd met someone who might help her get a foot in Hollywood's door, and that someone . . . well, she didn't quite know what to make of her encounter with Jared Taylor. "I like you, Klein," he'd said. What did that mean? Probably nothing. Christians are supposed to love everybody. Do they have to like everybody, too? *I hope not*, she thought. What a drag. At any rate, the whole experience had been painless, in stark contrast to her previous forays into the curious catacombs of religion . . . like the bus trip she'd taken at age thirteen to visit her cousin in Albany.

"Salvation! Do you believe in it?" The old man with loose dentures and halitosis repeated from the seat next to her.

Lori stared out the bus window and pretended not to hear. A bony elbow to her ribs persuaded her this ploy was useless. She suddenly hated her cousin for inviting her to visit, her mother for insisting she go, and Greyhound Bus Lines for just being there.

"I said, do you believe in salvation?"

I don't know, do I? Lori wondered. She managed a thin smile and nodded to her seatmate.

"Do you think I'm a believer?" he wheezed at her.

I thought you'd never ask.

"I'm here to tell you I'm a believer," he went on.

Good, I was afraid you had a bus fetish.

"Divine healing! I wouldn't be here today without it."

Too bad you didn't get your teeth fixed, too.

"Four years I suffered. Then I was delivered."

U.P.S.?

"Do you think I'm a believer?" he repeated.

I'm sorry, that question has already been used.

"Bells Palsy. I had Bells Palsy."

You should've given it back to Mr. Bell.

"But I'm here today."

This would be a wonderful story for the Reader's Digest.

The man continued to tell and retell his inspirational story for the duration of the trip to Albany.

Lori swore a solemn oath never to ride another bus— a vow she kept.

Jared found himself smiling as he pondered his afternoon encounter with Lori Klein. What in the world had attracted him to this rude, sarcastic, self-proclaimed atheist?

Well, in the fist place, she wasn't ugly. Not even close.

Secondly, she was clever, and Jared valued cleverness. He was drawn to people with whom he could verbally joust, someone who could return a witty lob with an overhead smash. Jared recognized that this was a failing of his. A clever person might be more fun at parties, but there was no genuine merit in slick repartee. Even so, he found predictable people boring.

Lastly, be it puppies or people, Jared was a rescuer. He knew that in spite of her brash talk and arrogant manner, Lori Klein was no match for the predators roaming Tinseltown.

• *FIVE* •

At home Jared hurried to change clothes for work. "Home" was a seven-unit complex in Burbank which he and his father owned. Jared lived in one of the apartments and acted as manager, maintenance man, and father confessor to the tenants of the other units.

As Jared drove up in front of his apartment building, he saw a large mongrel dog lying amid the contents of an overturned trash can and chewing on a disposable diaper. Seeing Jared, the animal placed his chin over his front paws and nervously twitched his tail, awaiting his fate.

"Did you do this?!" Jared yelled at the dog angrily, surveying the mess. "Huh? Did you?!"

The dog rolled over to beg mercy. Jared shook his head and went to get a rake.

"You've got real class, Maynard," he said.

The animal rushed to him now and lay at his feet, pleading for absolution. Jared gave him a couple of rough pats on the shoulder.

"You mangy mutt," he muttered affectionately.

The dog sprang to his feet and rushed madly about, demonstrating the joy that forgiveness brings.

Maynard adored Jared and would do anything for him except, of course, obey. Jared didn't really consider the animal his. He had fed Maynard one day when the dog showed up tired and hungry, and the beast decided to stick around and show his gratitude. Now Jared was buying dog food in forty-pound bags. Two at a time, and often.

As Jared cleaned up the litter, a cab stopped at the curb, and a middle-aged woman slowly emerged. Her head was bandaged, both eyes were swollen, and one arm was in a sling. She paid the driver, and as she turned, Jared recognized Margaret Morales, one of the tenants of the building.

"Good grief, Maggie! What happened?"

The woman glanced up, but didn't answer. Jared put one arm gently around her shoulder and with his free hand, took her heavy purse.

"Eddie beat me up," she said.

"Where's Eddie now?" Jared asked.

"In jail."

"I hope they throw away the key."

Maggie stopped and said, "A man does crazy things for the woman he loves."

Jared didn't know whether to laugh or cry.

"If Eddie Turner gets any crazier with you, Mag, you're not going to be around to love anymore."

"Eddie's a wonderful man when he's sober," Maggie said as they walked slowly toward her apartment.

"The problem is, it's hard to catch him in that condition," Jared said.

"You're a boy, Jared. You know nothing about love."

Margaret always talked down to Jared. This usually amused or annoyed him, depending on his mood. Today it did neither. Stopping at her apartment, he fished her keys from the purse, unlocked the door, and pushed it open.

"Are you hungry?" he asked her.

"No."

"When did you eat last?"

"Yesterday."

Jared walked into the kitchen and took some cottage cheese

and half a can of soup out of the refrigerator. He emptied the soup into a sauce pan.

"I'd like some coffee," Maggie said.

He washed out a pan that was in the sink, filled it with water, and put both containers on the range to heat.

Margaret sat at the small kitchen table and stared out the window. Jared put a jar of instant coffee and a cup on the table.

"You're a good boy, Jared."

He returned to the range and stirred the soup.

"Margaret, why don't you get rid of that bum?"

There was no response from the woman.

"He's nothing but trouble, Mag. You don't need that. It's stupid to keep seeing him."

"He's all I got," she said in a flat voice. "You got your family, Jared, and your church. I got nothing. Nothing but Eddie."

Eddie's worse than nothing, Jared thought, but he didn't say that because Maggie was crying. As she stared out the window, the tears ran down her cheeks onto her blood-stained slacks. He came and sat opposite her at the small table.

"I'm sorry, Maggie," he said as he reached across the table and covered her right hand with his. Jared wasn't exactly sure what he was sorry about. Certainly not for calling Eddie a bum. *I must be sorry that I made her cry,* he reasoned. But he wasn't sure that he had made her cry. Maybe she would have cried anyway.

Suddenly she grasped his hand in both of hers and held it so tightly that her fingernails dug into his flesh. She was crying hard now, her tears punctuated by muffled sobs. The soup was boiling, and Jared's hand was turning purple in her vise-like grip. It seemed, however, an inopportune moment for pointing out mundane matters like boiling cream of chicken or gangrene setting in on one's arm. *Eddie's the one who ought to have gangrene,* Jared thought. *In the head. And they should amputate.*

The crying began to subside, and the death grip relaxed.

"I need to go," Jared said as he slowly retrieved his arm.

"You're a good boy, Jared," Maggie repeated.

He went to the range and turned off the heat, gingerly flexing his mangled limb to see if it still functioned. Jared put the soup and hot water on the table.

"I'm going to work now. If you need anything, call Mrs. Stein. I'll talk to her before I leave."

"I'll be okay."

"Margaret?"

She looked up at Jared.

"You deserve someone better than Eddie. God loves you and wants you to be happy."

She shook her head slightly.

"He does, Mag. He loves you and wants to be your friend."

"I haven't lived a good life, Jared."

"You can change that, Maggie. You don't have to go on like this."

"When I was a girl, I went to Mass every week. Then my mother died, and I stopped going. I stopped believing."

"I'm going to ask a couple of ladies from my church to come over and see you, Margaret."

"All right," she said quietly.

"I'll talk to you later," he said, walking toward the door.

"Jared?"

He stopped and looked at her.

"What about Eddie?"

"What about him?" he asked, not liking the question.

"Doesn't God love Eddie, too?"

"I suppose so," Jared reluctantly agreed.

"He needs help, Jared," she pleaded.

"I know," he answered, feeling a little ashamed.

"Will you help him?"

"I can't help him, Maggie. Eddie's got to help himself."

"Would you try?"

There was a pause, then a brief sigh.

"I'll talk to him."

• *SIX* •

"Miss Klein?" asked the low, raspy voice on the phone.

"This is Lori Klein."

"Miss Klein, your name has been selected as the second place winner in our grand sweepstakes drawing."

"Who is this?"

"As the second place winner, you will be given an all expenses paid trip to Barstow," the voice scratched on.

Lori wasn't sure she heard correctly. "Where?" she asked in disbelief.

"Beauteous Barstow! The showplace of the West, the gathering place of the stars."

"Who is this?!" Lori insisted.

The voice was laughing now.

"Is this the creep? The Mormon creep?"

"Ha! You guessed the mystery voice! That means you win first prize! Which is a trip to the beach with the Mormon of your choice!"

"Why are you calling me at six a.m.?"

"It's actually 6:08."

"Why are you calling me at 6:08?"

"To ask you to go to the beach with me."

There was a pause.

"When?"

"Today. When's your last class?"

"It's over at three."

"Should I come by your apartment about 3:30?"

"Sure, what shall I bring?"

"Just a swim suit, a towel, and some grubby clothes."

"Are you going to feed me? I'll be starving."

"It's possible. Depends on your attitude."

"I'll be on my best behavior."

"That probably won't be good enough."

"See you at 3:30, Creep."

Jared finished the remodeling job on Mrs. Gibb's kitchen by one o'clock and sat for several minutes admiring his work. The cabinets especially pleased him. He loved working with wood. The aroma and variety, the way it felt and looked as it was shaped, sanded, and stained always gave him a good feeling.

He was alone in the house. Marquita, the housekeeper, was grocery shopping, and Mrs. Gibb was gone again for the day. She hadn't spoken to Jared since their confrontation the previous week. That suited Jared, though he worried that his comments to her had been a little extreme.

The job had been a giant pain. Each day Mrs. Gibb had changed her mind about how she wanted the work done. The changes were usually something minor, like moving a wall two or three feet one direction or another. "If this keeps up, I'll still be here during the Millennium," Jared had mumbled to himself.

Jared always made a sketch of the proposed changes and then explained the additional costs involved. Mrs. Gibb would balk at this, feigning poverty and accusing Jared of taking advantage of a poor widow. The "poor widow" was living in a Brentwood house worth over two mil and lavishly furnished from the assets of the late Henry Gibb. Jared decided early in his relationship with Althea Gibb that Henry had probably departed this earth of his own volition to escape the purgatory of life with Althea.

"Mrs. Gibb," Jared said at their final confrontation, "I'm not making any more changes. This is it. If you ask me to make one more change, I'm going to take this saw," he pointed to his circular saw, "and cut off my head. Then I'm going to run all over your house flapping my arms and gushing blood like a decapitated chicken. It won't be pleasant . . . for either of us."

Jared was pleased with the reaction to his little speech. Mrs. Gibb stood, her mouth ajar, and fixed him with a glassy, incredulous gaze. Then she backed slowly out of the room and left the house. Jared spent the remainder of the afternoon rehearsing what he would say when the police arrived. Fortunately, he didn't have to use that speech.

Thereafter, he was admitted to the house by Marquita, with whom he exchanged friendly banter and practiced his limited Spanish. The lady of the house was sometimes seen, but she didn't speak. Althea Gibb wanted nothing to do with a suicidal maniac. Anyone who threatened to bloody her Persian rugs was as dangerous as he was contemptible.

Having successfully gotten Mrs. Gibb off his back, Jared wondered playfully about writing a self-help book applying his new-found knowledge. Several titles were considered. *How to Lose Friends and Alienate People*, *The Jared Principle*, and *You're Okay, I'm Crazy* were among the competitors, but he finally decided on *The Power of Positive Paranoia*. That had a nice ring to it.

Jared loaded his tools in the pickup and cleaned up the sawdust and wood scraps. There was a check for him on the dining room table. This surprised him, knowing Mrs. Gibb's penchant for tight-fistedness. She had apparently decided that this was not a man to trifle with and that the sooner he was out of her life the better.

Jared changed his clothes, drove to the market for supplies, and then hurried on to Lori's.

• *SEVEN* •

"What's this?" Lori demanded as Jared led her outside. "You're taking me out in a truck?"

"This is no ordinary truck, Miss Klein. This magnificent piece of machinery is my work truck."

"Wow," she remarked dryly.

"I knew you'd be impressed. Do you like my new camper shell?"

"That's *new*?"

"Well, actually a friend of mine bought a new one and gave me his old one."

"Do you go to this much trouble for all the girls you date?"

"Just the rich ones."

"Who said I was rich?"

"All Jews are rich. Everyone knows that."

"All Mormons are crazy," Lori mumbled as he opened the door, and she climbed in.

"How was your week?" he asked as they drove down Westwood Boulevard toward Wilshire.

"Okay. I'm learning my way around L.A. a little better. If you get on the wrong freeway in this town, you're liable to end up in Nevada."

Jared laughed. "I grew up here, so I've never had much trouble."

Driving west on Wilshire, Jared turned onto the San Diego Freeway.

"Where are we going?" Lori asked.

"Laguna."

"Laguna? Is that close?"

"No, but it's nice."

They traveled for awhile without talking. Jared glanced over at her a few times, but she seemed engrossed in the surrounding suburbia. Eventually, their eyes met. She smiled and asked, "What are you thinking?"

"I'm thinking what a pretty girl you are. And what a terrific smile you have."

Lori looked out the window again.

"I was surprised when you called this morning," she said after a few moments.

"Pleasantly?" Jared asked.

She looked over and flashed her terrific smile but said nothing.

"I was surprised that I didn't call you sooner," he told her.

"Why didn't you?"

"I was afraid that you might say no. I can't stand rejection. I usually attempt suicide if a girl refuses to go out with me. Once I threw myself in front of a tall building and waited for an earthquake."

Lori tried to suppress a smile. Jared went on, "Another time I laid down in a supermarket freezer and pretended I was a package of broccoli."

"You should've tried the chopped liver section," Lori said.

Jared laughed.

"You're incredible, Klein."

It took just over an hour to get to Laguna Beach. Jared stopped at the entrance of a private residential area where a uniformed guard emerged from the booth at the gate.

"Hi, Bert!"

"Jared! Long time no see. How are you?"

"Good. How about you?"

"Fine. Really fine."

Introductions were made, and Bert waved them through with the admonition to have a good time and return soon.

Jared drove another quarter of a mile and parked in a cul-de-sac on a cliff overlooking the ocean. A few sailboats dotted the horizon and half a dozen surfers sat astride their boards waiting for the right wave.

"It's beautiful," Lori said. "Is this where your family lived?"

"No. I did some work for a couple of people who live here. You hungry?"

"Famished."

"Let's cook dinner."

"Cook? I've got to cook?"

"No. I'll cook. You get to bus."

Jared got the ice chest and a box of wood out of the truck. He handed Lori the wood, and they descended the steps to the beach below.

Several children were playing at the water's edge, throwing wet sand at each other and racing the breakers in and out. A small, tan girl in a yellow sunsuit was meticulously constructing a sand castle. Her grandmother sat nearby in a lounge chair, guarding the structure against vandalism. The sunbathers had retired for the day. One family was enjoying a wiener roast.

Jared and Lori stopped at a fire pit well away from the water. Jared took two foil-wrapped potatoes from the chest and buried them in the ashes.

"What are you doing?" Lori asked him.

"Putting our potatoes in the oven. Bring the wood here."

He placed the wood, along with some briquets, in the pit, poured lighter fluid over it, and set it aflame.

"Turn the thermostat to 425 please," he told Lori.

"Have you done this before?"

"Of course. How do you think I earned my cooking merit badge?"

"A Boy Scout," she said, shaking her head. "My mother would never believe this."

He smiled.

"Want to go for a swim?"

"Is it cold?" she asked.

"A little, but this is the best time to go. The sun's been warming the water all day. I'll go change."

Jared ran back to the truck, climbed beneath the shell, and changed into his swim trunks. Lori already had her suit on beneath her clothes. When Jared returned, he was carrying a duffel bag in one hand and a guitar in the other.

Lori watched his casual, fluid movements as he descended the steps three at a time. Her feelings about this sandy-haired young man with a little boy's smile were disturbing. She felt so comfortable with him. He seemed like a very old friend instead of a very new one. Silence between them was never awkward, conversation never forced. *Be careful, Lori Klein,* she thought. *You have a lot of plans for your life, and none of them include this Mormon Boy Scout.*

"Wow!" Jared exclaimed appreciatively, seeing her lithe, graceful figure in the close-fitting, one-piece suit.

She blushed a little, which surprised her.

"You like? I bought it this morning."

"Just for me?"

She shook her head. "Too small for you."

As they walked toward the water, their hands brushed, then clasped.

"Can you surf?" Lori asked.

"Sure, would you like to learn?"

"Did you bring a surf board?"

"Real surfers don't use boards, Klein. If the Lord had intended for man to surf on a board, he would've made him out of polyurethane and epoxy. Body surfing is the one true art form."

"You're crazy."

"Come on."

They waded out above their knees, and Jared explained

about diving beneath the breakers to keep from being tossed around. Then they swam out to deeper water. Lori was a good swimmer, cutting through the water with swift, sure strokes.

"Stop here," Jared said after they had gone a short distance where the water was about four feet deep between swells.

"What you do," he explained, "is start swimming like mad just as the wave starts to break. You want to get on top of it. Then you just kind of slide down the front and ride it in. The trick is knowing when to swim. If you start too late, you'll miss it; and if you start too soon, the wave will flip you over and bounce you around like a football. If that happens, try to relax. Watch me take one."

As the grey-green swell moved toward them, Jared edged inward a few feet; then, just as the wave reached its crest, he threw his body toward the shore, kicking hard, and gave three furious strokes. Jared disappeared for an instant, then Lori saw his head bouncing and bobbing toward the beach. He emerged whooping and shouting, then swam back to where Lori was waiting.

They stood together, rejecting several small waves. Then Jared announced, "Okay, Klein, here's a good one. Let's move out a little. Right here. Now take off when I tell you . . . Go!"

They bumped shoulders as the wave crashed and swept them to shore side by side.

"You did it, Klein! That's fantastic! It took me weeks to learn that."

"That's because you're a klutz," she said triumphantly. "Besides," she began to giggle, "I learned to body surf when I was sixteen."

Jared gave her the most disgusted look he could muster before he joined in her laughter.

They rode waves in together several times, then Lori caught one that Jared missed.

"Hey, what happened, Surf King?" she teased as she returned.

"Too small," he responded, pretending nonchalance.

"You can't cut it, Mormon," she taunted.

"You're washed up. This beach isn't big enough for both of us."

"Okay, Champ, let's see what you can do with this one," he said, pointing to an ominous-looking swell closing in on them. "I'm riding this all the way to my truck. Let's go!"

Lori took off swimming, and Jared tucked his knees to his chest and dropped to the ocean floor, letting the wave sweep over him. When he came up, Lori was rolling sideways toward shore. She finally grabbed a handful of sand and staggered to her feet.

"Too soon, Klein!" came a happy shout. "You left too soon!"

"Creep! Lousy, rotten creep!" Lori yelled.

Lori stood and watched while Jared hitched onto a friendly breaker and surfed toward her. When he came within range, she hit him square in the face with a clump of seaweed and took off running up the beach.

Jared just laughed and turned back to the water to wash off his face.

"Come on, Klein, let's eat!"

She joined him at the fire pit where he placed a grate over the coals and put the meat on it.

"How do you like your steaks?"

"Steaks? I'm impressed, Taylor. Medium well."

They dried off and sat down on the blanket that had appeared from Jared's duffel bag. He handed her a small bowl of fruit salad.

"This is good," Lori said.

"I got it at Pasquale's. His wife made it."

"They should open up a restaurant."

"I'll tell them you said so."

When the steaks were ready, Jared dug the potatoes out of the hot coals. They were a little too chewy in the middle, but neither of the diners seemed to mind. The two sat across from each other on the blanket, using the ice chest as a table.

As they finished eating, a light breeze began blowing in from the ocean. Jared stood and got two sweat shirts from the bag and handed one to Lori.

"Thanks," she said as she stood up. "Let's go for a walk."

They walked along the water's edge, holding hands and talking quietly, stopping occasionally to examine a shell or a sand dollar. One of the sweat shirts had "BYU" printed on it.

"Did you go to BYU?" Lori asked.

"Uh-huh. I went there for two years. Then I went on my mission for the Church.

"Why didn't you go back to school?"

"Well, Dad was leaving the country, and he needed me here to look after some property that he owns. Also, I'd already decided that I wanted to build houses and write for a living. I don't need a degree to do either of those things. I'm taking a couple of writing classes. So do you have plans besides acting?"

"Actually, I'm already an actress, but I'm going to be a star. I want my footprints in the cement outside Mann's Chinese Theater."

"Fame and fortune, huh?"

"Is there anything wrong with that?" she asked defensively, not liking the tone of his comment.

"I think it's a poor substitute for happiness."

"And what, Oh Great One, is the true source of happiness? Getting married and having babies, I suppose."

"Well, I think that would be preferable to having babies and not getting married."

Lori frowned. "Seriously, is that what you think?"

"Lori, I know something about the movie business. Most of the power is in the hands of ruthless, degenerate people. They're bright, creative, exciting people, but their morals are in the sewer. The price of success can be high. Really high. Especially for an actress."

"Where do I write for a copy of this sermon?"

"I'm sorry. I didn't mean to preach. I just care what happens to you."

"I'm a big girl."

"I think you're just the right size."

The sun was dropping into the water, painting the waves pink and gold. Jared put his arm around Lori's shoulders. She leaned against him and put her arm around his waist, and they walked back toward the fire.

"Ready for dessert?" Jared asked when they arrived at the fire pit.

"Certainly. I'll have the chocolate mousse, please."

"I'm sorry, that's an endangered species. But you'll love the s'mores."

Jared opened a plastic bag of marshmallows, and then the box of graham crackers.

"Get the Hershey bars out of the ice chest, will you?" he asked Lori.

Jared impaled a marshmallow on a former coat hanger and held it carefully over the glowing coals.

"Put a piece of chocolate on one of the graham crackers," Jared ordered.

When she complied, he placed the roasted marshmallow atop the candy and sandwiched it with another cracker, smashing the hot marshmallow over the chocolate.

"Eat, my child."

They ate five s'mores each, taking turns knocking each other's marshmallows off the coat hanger into the fire and commenting critically on the culinary aptitude of certain Jews and Mormons.

"Is it time for the concert now?" Lori asked, nodding toward Jared's guitar.

"Ah, yes, the moment we've all been waiting for," he said, grabbing the instrument. "Ladies and gentlemen," he went on, "let's give a warm welcome to the incredibly talented and wonderfully humble Mr. Jared Taylor!"

Lori gave two claps.

Jared sang a silly song called "I'm a Sucker for a Girl Like That," then did "King of the Road." Lori joined in the second number, singing harmony. Then she took the guitar and began to play. Jared just sort of strummed a guitar, but Lori played it.

"That's why you wanted to get to the concert," he protested. "So you could make me look bad."

"It wasn't hard," she replied, smiling sweetly.

"You're brutal, Klein."

They took turns strumming and playing, singing together and separately, doing silly songs solemnly and making up ludicrous lyrics to serious pieces. Gradually the music gave way to conversation. About eleven o'clock, Jared reluctantly said, "Better go, huh?"

"I guess so," she nodded.

The drive home was quiet. At the door to her apartment, Lori turned and gazed into Jared's face.

"I had a super time," she said.

He leaned forward and kissed her gently.

"Is that any way for a Boy Scout to act?" She asked softly.

"A scout is friendly," he reminded her.

"Thanks for the warning."

"I'll call you."

"When?"

"When I get home."

"Why not sooner?"

"I don't have a quarter."

"Get one."

Jared got off the freeway in Panorama City and called her from an all-night coffee shop.

"What are you doing tomorrow night?" he asked.

"I've got a date with a Mormon truck driver."

"Is he going to take you to a Neil Simon play in Glendale?"

"Probably."

"Do you suppose he'll pick you up about six-thirty?"

"I think so."

"You're a very lucky girl. I'll bet you'll have a terrific evening."

"I doubt it," she said and hung up.

• *EIGHT* •

The theater seated over four hundred people, and the place was full. It was a theater in the round, with the audience closely surrounding the stage. The play was well done, and afterwards Jared introduced her to the owner of the playhouse, an impeccably dressed, distinguished looking man in his sixties with a bumper crop of curly silver hair.

"Hello, Nate."

"Jared! How are you?"

"Pretty good."

"How are your parents doing in Australia?"

"Fine. Nate, this is Lori Klein, a friend of mine—an actress."

"Well, I'm pleased to meet you, Lori."

"She's interested in reading for one of your plays."

"Well," he repeated, "let's go upstairs to my office, and I'll give you a schedule of what's coming up."

Upstairs, the silver-haired man got a report on every member of the Taylor family and proudly gave information on his offspring and their offspring. Finally he got around to Lori.

"Tell me about yourself, young lady."

She recited her credits, and the man listened politely.

"How do you like our theater?" he asked.

"It's really lovely."

"Let me show you around," he offered.

They were shown the rehearsal hall, the dressing rooms, the costume section, and the control room. He explained how he and his young family had come to Los Angeles from a small town in Northern Utah during World War II.

"I read in the newspaper that there was a dearth of leading men in Hollywood because of the war," he chuckled, "so I came out here to be a star. I delivered milk in the morning and acted in a little theater at night. My wife, Ruth, wrote a play for the Church about a schoolteacher who came from the city to our little valley in Utah to teach. We rented an old house on Colorado Boulevard to rehearse in. We put some folding chairs in the house and began showing the play on Fridays and Saturdays. That was the beginning. Eventually, we built a two-hundred seat theater and finally, this one."

"Nate, Lori would like to be in one of your plays," Jared gently reminded him.

"Of course! Let me talk to Ruth. We'll find a good play for you. Maybe something you could sing in. Why don't you call me in about a week?"

"I don't want any special favors, Mister . . ."

"Nonsense! If Jared says that you have talent, I'm sure that you'd be ideal in one of our productions."

"I didn't say she had talent," Jared teased.

"Well, I'm sure that she does. Now you young people run along and have a nice evening."

"Is he one of the vicious degenerates that you warned me about?" Lori asked as they walked toward the car.

"Nate's not exactly a Hollywood mogul, Klein."

"Really?" she smiled. "I'm honored that you didn't bring your work truck tonight," she said, getting into his VW.

"For formal occasions, I prefer the limo."

"I've never ridden in a limousine."

"Poor baby, it must've been terrible for you."

They drove to a nearby Marie Callendar's to eat. The parking lot was packed, but a car near the entrance was preparing to leave. Jared waited while the elderly driver backed slowly out and laboriously turned the steering wheel toward the exit.

While this was being accomplished, a silver Porsche wheeled around both cars and zipped into the newly-vacated parking space. A broad shouldered man with no neck emerged with a confident smirk. He was joined by his date, a Dolly Parton pretender, who was giggling and squeezing his arm to congratulate him on his heroic deed.

Lori gave them an angry stare as the obnoxious couple strolled toward the restaurant. Jared seemed detached, as if pondering what to do next. When they were opposite the VW, the reckless man turned and gave Jared and Lori an exaggerated wink.

"He shouldn't have done that," Jared said.

"Don't fight him. He could be rabid," Lori warned.

"Go put our name on the waiting list. I'll join you in a few minutes."

Jared had to park over half a block away. Jogging back toward the restaurant, he suddenly slowed his pace as he noticed a figure dressed in dark clothing crouching beside the offending Porsche. Jared observed the man for a moment and concluded that he was trying to break into the car. He thought for a few seconds, then crept quietly up behind the man and jabbed two fingers sharply in his back.

"Freeze!" Jared said sternly.

The man dropped a huge ring of keys and shot both hands into the air. "Don't shoot!" He pleaded. "I'm a Repo man. Payments on this car are five months overdue. I got papers. Honest!"

"Where?" Jared grunted. He was getting into the role.

"In my back pocket. Take a look."

Jared retrieved some papers from the man's pocket, glanced quickly through them, then laid them on the roof of the car.

"Be my guest," Jared said, turning to go.

"You a cop?" the Repo man asked Jared.

"No. You a crook?"

The man didn't exactly answer the question, but he did have some very uncomplimentary things to say about Jared Taylor and the scare he had received by those two fingers sticking in his back.

Inside the restaurant, Jared led Lori to a room where they could look out the window and see the Porsche portion of the parking lot. He explained to her what was going on and they watched in delight as the Repo man did his duty.

The reckless one and his date were just digging into their prime rib when the waiter delivered an envelope to his table. The bewildered man opened it and a dollar bill fell out, along with a note which read:

Dear Sir,
   Kindly use the enclosed $ to call yourself a cab. Your automobile has been repossessed.
Sincerely Yours,
Jared & Lori

• *NINE* •

The next few weeks were a blur, a blissful montage of places and events. There was a concert at Royce Hall, a BYU-UCLA football game, and a visit to the Magic Castle, an old Hollywood mansion that had been converted to a private club for magicians and their guests.

"Would you like to go water skiing Saturday?" Jared asked one afternoon.

"Sure. Do you have a boat?"

"No, I'm going to borrow my brother-in-law's boat and take my Sunday School class up to Lake Pyramid."

"Your Sunday School class!" Jared couldn't miss a marked lack of enthusiasm in her tone.

"You'll love it, Klein. There'll be a dozen or so twelve and thirteen-year-olds."

"I think I'll wish I'd stayed home," she said.

"But you won't."

"You're certainly sure of yourself."

"I'm irresistible company," he assured her.

Everyone met in the parking lot of the church Saturday morning. Although they had planned to leave at 7:30 sharp, it was a little after 8:00 by the time they got on the road.

Jared had borrowed Dave Jennings' camper, along with

the boat, and Clyde Putnam, a member of the bishopric, brought his station wagon to handle the overflow. Sixteen kids showed up—which didn't include Clyde's seven-year-old daughter, Kelly, who decided to ride in the cab of the truck with Jared and Lori.

Clyde Putnam called on one of the kids to offer a prayer, then they scrambled for the vehicles. Naturally, everyone wanted to ride in the camper.

"Hayes, Luke, Alison, Vicki, and Jessica go ride in the station wagon," Jared ordered.

"That's not fair, Brother Taylor!" one of the girls protested. "We were here before Megan and Elisha!"

"Tough," Jared replied democratically. Then he added, "You can ride in the camper on the way home."

"All right!" they replied almost as one.

"That'll be better anyway. That way we can sleep," added one of the boys.

"Okay, listen everybody!" Jared called to those riding with him. "This is not my camper. If it were, I wouldn't let any of you animals near it." That proclamation brought a few guffaws and some moos from the male livestock.

"Is this the rig that belongs to that rich movie dude?" a doe-eyed blonde asked.

"That's right, and he expects it back in the same condition that it's in right now."

"You better not let Russell ride in it then," offered a freckled boy with glasses.

"Why don't you just shut up, Four Eyes!" came a surly reply from a heavy-set boy in the bunk over the cab.

"Hey, Russell! Maybe that movie guy would put you in one of his horror flicks!" persisted the boy.

"You better shut up, you freckle-faced idiot!"

"Okay, cool it! Both of you. Or you'll be staying home. Is that clear?" Jared warned.

The freckled-face boy smiled an impish grin and boarded the camper. Jared looked at Lori and shook his head. "If that kid lives through puberty, it'll be a miracle."

"What's puberty?" the boy demanded.

"Never mind."

"Is it dirty?" he asked hopefully.

"Just get in the truck, will you?"

The trip to the lake was largely uneventful. Craig Metcalf prudently decided not to further antagonize Russell Sax because the camper afforded very little running room.

Little Kelly Putnam studied Lori as they drove. Lori glanced over at her a few times and smiled, but the little girl's intent expression remained unchanged.

"Are you a girl?" she asked finally.

"Uh . . . yes," Lori replied, somewhat mystified.

"You don't have zits," she said accusingly.

"Well . . . not with me."

"My sister says when a girl grows up, she gets zits. Lots of 'em," Kelly pursued.

Lori was unsure how to respond to that. She glanced over at Jared, who was having a difficult time controlling his mirth and the truck at the same time. She shot him a sharp left elbow to the ribs, and the fine thread holding his composure came unraveled.

"Brother Taylor will now explain that to you, Kelly," Lori announced.

"Oh, yeah, sure, I'd be glad to," Jared said when he was more or less able to speak again. "You see . . . Kelly . . ."

Now it was Lori's turn to watch *him* squirm. "Well, it's like this. Lori is not really a girl," He cracked up again. "Actually," he went on, "she's a woman. That's it. Yes, a woman. And when a girl becomes a woman . . . she loses her zits!" he said triumphantly.

Kelly pondered the ramifications of this newfound knowledge. Then she nodded sagely, indicating that she found the arrangement satisfactory.

* * *

Taking sixteen kids water skiing with one boat is something less than total joy. Only three had ever skied before, so the task of getting everyone "up" before sundown was a formidable one. Lori marveled at the patience shown by Clyde Putnam and Jared as the two men taught the kids to ski. Clyde was a huge, affable man who walked with short, shuffling steps and carried a permanent smile pursed on his lips, as though he harbored some private joke.

Jared and Clyde gave group instruction, which each skier promptly forgot when it was his turn to ski. Then there was individual instruction, which most either forgot or ignored when they were in the water and the boat started to pull. Then there was re-instruction and encouragement until it was done right.

Two of the girls who hadn't skied before got up on the first try. Heidi, the doe-eyed blonde, only went about fifty yards before falling, but Alison, a tall, confident brunette, popped up and skied all over the lake like it was something she did every day.

Russell Sax stayed apart from the rest of the group. He pretended to be too busy looking at the lake bottom through his face mask to want to ski. Clyde called to him a couple of times, but the boy shook his head and dived beneath the water to examine the mud. Finally Jared shouted, "Hey, Russ! Come on, I'll let you drive the boat while I ski."

"All right!" came the immediate reply.

This sparked dissent among the gathering. Russell was not a popular boy.

"Hey! How come he gets to drive?" several demanded.

"Now wait!" Jared held up his hands for silence. "The laws of the State of California clearly state that a boy who is nearly fourteen years old can drive a boat if he's accompanied by his Sunday School teacher and he owns a snorkel and face-mask!"

"You lie, Brother Taylor!" Heidi said.

Russell climbed happily into the boat, and Jared ordered everyone else out except for Kelly. Then he asked Lori to join them.

They went for a test ride while Russell got the feel of the boat.

"Punch it all the way, then back off a little as soon as I'm up," Jared explained after they stopped mid-lake. Donning the ski vest, he jumped overboard, and Lori handed him a ski.

"Do you want both skis?" she asked.

"No, with a great driver like Russ I'll pop right up on one."

Lori rolled her eyes heavenward, but said nothing. Russell was the picture of concentration—a P.T. boat skipper tracking an enemy sub.

"When I get up, take me around the island, then drop me at the shore over by the dam," Jared said.

"Why over there?" Lori asked.

"Because," came the cryptic reply.

Jared skied around the island, then dropped off and swam into shore where he waited for the boat to return. This was a remote part of the lake, and there was only one other boat on the small beach.

"How'd I do, Brother Taylor?" Russell shouted when the boat motored into shore.

"Terrific, Russ! I had a great ride."

Russell's huge smile threatened to meet at the back of his head.

"Okay, it's your turn to ski now, Russ," Jared said.

The smile disappeared in a flash. "No, I don't want to. I'd rather drive."

"Russell, you're going to ski."

"No. No, I can't, Brother Taylor. I'm too clumsy."

"Who says?"

Russell shrugged his shoulders and looked at his feet.

"Russ, you can ski. You can ride a bike, can't you?"

"Sure. Anybody can ride a bike."

"If you can ride a bike, you can ski."

Russell thought about that for a moment.

"I'm going to tell you exactly what to do. You probably won't make it the first couple of times, but you'll get up. And when you do, we're going to take you right past our group across the lake over there. And Craig Metcalf is going to say, 'Who is that out there? It's a bird! It's a plane! It's Russell Sax!'"

Russell was giggling in anticipation now.

"And Carla Wilson," Jared went on. "You know what beautiful Carla's going to say when she sees you out there? She's gonna say, 'Oh, Russell! You are so wonderful!'" He finished his little speech in a Miss Piggy falsetto, and Russell was already putting on the ski vest.

There were several false starts. After each one, Russell would quit, and Jared would begin anew—encouraging, prodding, teaching.

"Just let the boat do the work. Don't stand up too soon. You nearly had it that time."

Lori was holding the flag which indicates a skier is in the water, wondering what was so important about teaching this fat kid to ski. Then it came to her. It was important to Jared because that fat kid was important to Jared. And the way that kid felt about himself was important to Jared. She realized then that she could very well end up sitting in that stupid boat at midnight holding that stupid flag in the air, because Jared Taylor was not going to let that boy fail. Lori felt the sting of tears, and suddenly she too was rooting for Russell Sax. She also suddenly wanted very much to kiss Jared Taylor. She did, too, three tries later when Russell Sax became a water skier.

At dusk, Lori stood at the top of the boat ramp and watched as Clyde, Jared, and the boys put the boat back on the trailer. Kelly Putnam approached her. "Are you a Mormon?" she asked Lori.

"No."

"I guess you and Jared won't get married then?"

"Oh, why not?"

"'Cause, if you're not a Mormon, you can't go to the temple."

"What happens in the temple?" Lori asked.

"You get married forever."

"That's a long time," Lori said, smiling at the irony of a Jew not being able to go to the temple.

Kelly wandered off. Lori tried to dismiss the incident from her mind, but it wasn't ready to leave. She and Jared had avoided the subject of religion. They both knew why. Neither wanted to face that unpleasant issue. Neither was ready for that . . . not yet.

Jared and Lori rode alone in the cab of the truck driving home. "How do Mormons feel about dating non-Mormons?" she asked.

"I feel fine, how do you feel?" he replied.

She decided not to pursue the subject. "I don't think I can compete with all those beauties in your Sunday School class," she said.

"Don't let it get you down, Klein. You've got a few things going for you."

"Like what?" she asked.

Jared thought for several moments. "You don't have zits," he said.

• *TEN* •

"I'd like to see where you live," Lori said when Jared picked her up for lunch one day.

"Nah, I'd be embarrassed."

"Why?"

"It's too pretentious."

"Come on, Taylor. Take me to your litter."

"Okay. I'll fix us some lunch in my sumptuous kitchen. Do you like Mexican food?"

"Do you live with a Mexican chef?"

"Klein, I make an incredible burrito. In fact, as you should know, I cook even better than I play the guitar."

They stopped at a market for supplies and headed toward Burbank.

Jared gave Lori a brief biography of some of the occupants in his building on the trip over.

"In Apartment Number 1, we have Bernard and Bayla Stein, our token Jewish family. They've lived there for years. Moved here from New Jersey when he retired to be close to their daughter. Nice people. Bernie had a stroke a couple of months ago. He just came home last week from the hospital.

"Margaret Morales is in Apartment Five. She's the queen of the K-Mart checkers. Maggie's going with a wonderful guy named Eddie whose idea of a good time is to beat up on

Margaret. Do you know why?"

"Why?"

"Because, 'A man does crazy things for the woman he loves,'" Jared said in his best Maggie Morales accent.

"She said that?" Lori asked.

"She did."

"You're kidding!"

He went into the accent again. "You are a child, Jared. You know nothing of love."

"She didn't say that!"

Jared nodded his head, laughing.

"Sounds like a real soap opera."

"*All My Children*," Jared smiled, then becoming more serious, he said, "Maggie's had a tough life, though. Her mother died when she was young; she's been through a series of bad marriages and worse boyfriends. I feel sorry for her. She's trying to change. She went to church last Sunday."

"Your church?"

"Uh-huh."

"Is she a Mormon?"

"No."

"Mormons think everyone ought to be Mormon, don't they?"

"When you feel you have something good, you want to share it," Jared said simply.

Jared's street was in an old section of Burbank. The building was a U-shaped structure with three apartments on each side facing one another and one larger apartment in the rear, where Jared lived.

A bewildered-looking old man was standing on the walk between the two buildings when they drove up. He was wearing only a pajama top, boxer shorts, and brown shoes with no laces.

"Uh-oh." Jared got out of the car and walked quickly to the man. Lori joined them. "Bernie! What's the matter?"

The man made some unintelligible noises and pointed to

the front yard and then to his apartment. Jared strained to understand. The old man tried again. This time Jared deciphered part of the message.

"The paper?" Jared asked.

Bernie nodded and mumbled, pointing at his apartment.

"You came out to get the paper and got locked out?"

He nodded again.

"What's the idea of coming outside with no pants? You trying to get me arrested? They'll lock me up for renting an apartment to a pervert."

The old man made some strange little grunting sounds, and Lori realized that he was laughing.

"Here I am trying to impress this girl with what a high-class neighborhood I live in, and you're standing out here in your underwear!"

The short, wheezing grunts continued.

"You've disgraced the whole neighborhood, Bern. Brought shame and humiliation upon us all." Jared took his arm lightly and steered him toward his apartment.

Bernie tried to talk again.

"You couldn't get your pants on?" Jared repeated, and Bernie nodded. "I guess I should be grateful that you weren't standing out here in the buff! It's a good thing we're not in Hollywood, Bern. Some weirdo would probably come by and take your shoes."

Lori's feelings were strangely ambivalent as she watched this scene. Listening to this conversation between Bernard Stein and his landlord, she felt jealous that this feeble man was commanding Jared's full attention, while she was being ignored. She had felt the same way at the lake with his Sunday School class. That told her something about Lori Klein that she didn't like. She thought how little she really knew about Jared, yet witnessing this strange exchange between the old and the young, the weak and the strong, she realized that she loved him. The more she was with Jared, the less she understood him, but the more she loved him.

• *ELEVEN* •

Jared and Lori sat munching greasy taquitos in a small open patio on Olvera Street, supposedly L.A.'s oldest street, where tourists from all over the planet can gather to buy Mexican trinkets made in Hong Kong. Lori ate just a few bites, then pushed her plate away.

"I think the chef here could qualify for a job at Taylor Towers," she teased.

"You think you can say anything you want to me, don't you?"

"Yep," she smiled.

"Beautiful girls get away with murder."

Later the two of them strolled hand in hand through he cavernous innards of nearby Union Station.

"Have you ever ridden on a train?" Lori asked.

"Sure, haven't you?"

"No."

"Where would you like to go, Miss Klein?"

"Anywhere."

"That should be easy enough to arrange," Jared said, checking the large board overhead that gave the train arrival and departure times.

"How about leaving for San Diego in twenty minutes?"

"Are you serious?"

"Of course."

"We can't go to San Diego. What about school? What about your work?" Lori protested.

"What about it?"

"I don't even have a toothbrush, or a nightgown," Lori went on.

"I'll pop for a toothbrush. I have an aunt in La Jolla. We can stay with her tonight."

Jared purchased a tiny plastic ukulele, plus toothbrushes, deodorant, and a razor at a shop in the train station. They spent the trip down trying to tune the ukulele and get some music out of it, while enjoying the beauty of the coastline.

"Hello, Reet?"

"Jared?"

"How'd you know?"

"Because no one else calls me Reet. Where are you calling from?"

"San Diego. Where are you answering from?"

"What are you doing here?" Rita usually ignored Jared's banalities.

"I came down on the train with a friend. We'd like to come and take you out to dinner and spend the night."

"Certainly. I've already had dinner, though. Can I come and pick you up?"

"No, I'll rent a car. We'll take you out for dessert. How's that?"

"That's fine."

"Okay. See you in a while."

"Good-bye, Jared."

"Charlie, Rita's husband, died about nine years ago," Jared explained to Lori as they drove back up the coast toward La Jolla. "She lives alone. Teaches literature at San Diego State. A really super lady. I spent the summer with her when I was fourteen, after Charlie died."

"Does she have children?"

"Two daughters. One lives in Oceanside, which is close, and the other is in Arizona."

Jared and Lori picked Rita up, and she directed them to an old house that had been converted into a restaurant. Most of the conversation was handled by Jared and Rita. Lori was content to listen. She felt vaguely uncomfortable with the questions addressed to her by Jared's aunt. The woman seemed to be paying too much attention to her answers, listening for something that Lori had left unsaid. Still, she liked Rita. Lori felt a kind of unspoken kinship with her.

Back at Rita's comfortable beach house, Jared spent the night on a sofa in the den and Lori used the spare bedroom. She slept late the next morning and had little appetite for breakfast. After a swim, Jared and Lori drove into town and wandered through La Jolla's shops and galleries. Rita had no afternoon classes that day and insisted that they return to her house for a late lunch before heading back to San Diego to catch the train for Los Angeles.

"Jared, would you be a dear and go pick up a prescription for me at the drug store?" Rita inquired as they finished lunch.

"Sure."

"Why don't you stay and chat with me?" she said to Lori.

The girl sat obediently, feeling suddenly as if she were visiting the dentist.

"May I speak frankly with you?" Rita asked as soon as Jared had gone.

"Do you need my permission?" Lori answered defensively.

"Please don't tune me out. I want to help. Really, I do."

"I don't remember asking for your help."

"Are you in love with Jared?"

"I don't think that's any of your bus—"

"Because if you are," Rita interrupted, "you'll listen to what I have to say. Do you love him?"

"Yes," Lori answered softly. "I suppose I do."

"I thought so. Have the two of you talked of marriage?"

"No. I don't want to get married."

"What, then, do you want from this relationship? A lover?"

Lori flushed a little but didn't answer.

Rita continued, "That wouldn't work, Lori. In the first place, I doubt very much that Jared would enter into that kind of relationship with you outside of marriage. We simply don't believe in that. I know that sounds terribly old-fashioned, but that's how it is. Chastity is not a popular commandment, nor an easy one to live, especially for people in love, but those who keep it are never sorry.

"Jared is a joy to be with because he likes himself," Rita continued. "He doesn't wrestle with guilt and self-doubt. His conscience is clear. He's a special young man, largely because of his religion. He loves it, and he lives it. Do you know any-thing about Mormonism?"

"Well . . . a little. I don't really understand it," Lori answered.

"No, of course you don't. No one really understands Mormonism except for Mormons, and only about half of them. It's a way of life. A commitment to serve, to follow Christ. That commitment is an integral part of a Mormon's life. I simply can't see how you could successfully share his life without sharing that commitment. It would be impossible if you weren't married, and even if you were, you would resent the time that Jared spent away from you doing church work. And he would feel guilty if he didn't do it and guilty if he did. You want a career and a lover. He wants a wife and a family. How can those huge differences be resolved?"

Lori sat staring into space, biting her lip. Suddenly her eyes welled with tears, and the dam broke. Rita went and sat with her on the sofa. She put her arms around Lori and waited patiently for her crying to subside.

"What am I going to do?" Lori asked finally.

"I don't know, child. I don't know," Rita replied. "It was foolish of Jared to let this go so far. Cruel and foolish."

"He didn't 'let it go.' It just went. I don't think either of us was prepared for what's happened," Lori said through her tears.

"I know," Rita said apologetically. "One does not control the course of love."

"I don't think I could ever be a Mormon, Rita. The whole story seems so . . ."

"Unbelievable?"

"Yes," Lori nodded.

"I was raised a Mormon," Rita said. "My great, great maternal grandmother, Lillian Conrad, joined the Church in Scotland at seventeen and was promptly disowned by her parents. She emigrated to the United States and came across the plains with a handcart company. She battled Indians, crickets, and smallpox. She had thirteen children and lived to be ninety-one. I admired her courage and independence but found no need for her faith."

"What do you mean?"

"While I was a student at Stanford, I left the Church completely. Religion was the 'opiate of the masses,' a crutch for the weak, the uneducated. I prided myself in my intellectual independence. Then I met Charles. He saw me as the shallow conformist that I was. I was dwarfed by his intellect, amazed by his faith, and captivated by his charm. "Charles had studied for the Lutheran ministry and had visited Salt Lake City the summer after his junior year. After his visit, he decided to expose the fraudulent claims of Mormonism. He was baptized six weeks later. His conversion was complete, his commitment total. He went to England on a mission for two years, then came to Stanford to study law."

"Is that where you met?" Lori asked.

"Yes," she continued. "On our fourth date he said to me, 'Rita Wooley, it's time you learned that the gospel is true, so I can take you to the House of the Lord and make you mine for eternity.'" Rita smiled, remembering the moment. "So I went to work. It was a struggle. I felt like a hypocrite when I tried to pray. I couldn't get interested in the Book of Mormon, and I didn't understand the Bible. It was terrible. Charles encouraged me and answered many of my questions, but he made it clear that I had to find out for myself. He couldn't do it for me. Gradually, the pieces began to fall in place, my faith started to grow, and the answer came."

Lori looked forlorn and unconvinced.

"Think about it. You've nothing to lose and perhaps much to gain. Did Jared tell you about the summer he spent here?" Rita asked, trying to brighten things up.

"He mentioned it."

"That was a very painful time for me. Charles' death was so unexpected. He simply had a heart attack and was gone. It was inconceivable. He had scarcely been sick a day in his life. Both of the girls had already married. I was sick and alone. Jared's mother suggested that he spend his summer vacation here since he came every year anyway for a week or two. He loves the beach."

"I know."

"We had quite a time together. Every morning, the two of us would work in the yard. We planted a huge vegetable garden and had flowers everywhere. We built a fence around the backyard and a roof over the patio. He was a marvel. Afternoons we'd go to the beach. Jared would surf and play four-man volleyball, and I would read and sun myself.

"Soon he coaxed me into playing volleyball. I had been quite an athlete when I was younger. Well, before long that skinny boy and his old aunt were a couple of the best volleyball players in La Jolla. One day we beat two hot-shot football players from the College, much to their chagrin and the delight of their friends.

"Those three months were great therapy for me. They gave me the will to go on without Charles, to stop feeling sorry for myself and to get on with the business of living. I went back to school in the fall, got my doctorate, and was offered a position at SDS. I owe a great deal to Jared, though I'm sure that he never considered me in his debt," Rita said.

"You love him too, don't you?" Lori said.

"Oh, yes. Jared is the son that Charles and I were never blessed with. He's very special to me."

"Do you resent me?" Lori asked.

"No. Not at all. I think you're a delightful young woman. You remind me of Laura, Jared's mother. You'd like her. She's not at all stuffy like her older sister." Rita smiled at her little self-deprecating joke.

Lori managed a faint smile, too.

"I am worried, though," Rita continued. "It's glorious to be in love, but that's not enough. You need common goals and ideals, shared values. You and Jared don't have that, and the sooner the two of you face these issues and deal with them, the less pain both of you will have."

When Jared returned, he sensed at once that things were not as he had left them. Rita gave Lori a prolonged embrace as they left. "I'm here if you need me," she said. Rita also hugged Jared and then stood looking at him. "You're an impetuous fool," she said.

"I'm taking you out of my will, Reet."

She smiled and turned away, shaking her head.

Neither Jared nor Lori said much until the train was under-way. They sat close together, holding hands, her head on his shoulder.

"What did Rita say?" Jared asked.

"She wanted to know if I love you . . . I guess she thinks that you're in love with me."

"I guess she's right," he said quietly.

Lori took his face between her hands and smiled sadly. "That makes matters very complicated."

"Why?"

"Because I love you, too."

"That *is* bad," Jared joked.

"It's time to quit pretending, Jared."

"I know. I've been lying to myself for three weeks. Telling

myself that you didn't really matter that much to me—that I could walk away any time. Ever since I was a little kid, Lori, one of my goals has been to be married in a Mormon temple. We believe that marriage can be an eternal thing. It's sacred. Only worthy Mormons are allowed in the temple. Now I'm in love with someone who not only doesn't share my religious beliefs, but doesn't even believe in marriage."

"If that's a proposal," Lori said, fighting back the tears, "it's the lousiest one I ever heard!" She lost the fight.

"I'm sorry," Jared said helplessly.

"What is it you want from me? I'm supposed to forget about a career, become a Mormon, get married, stay home, and have kids? What do you plan to give up?"

Jared didn't try to answer. He just held her while she cried.

• *TWELVE* •

"Kenny?"

"Yes."

"Ken, this is Lori."

"Lori! Where are you?"

"California."

"Oh, that's what I thought. How's school?"

"Kenny, I'm pregnant."

"You . . . what?"

"Pregnant, Kenny. I'm going to have a baby."

"Well, why are you calling . . . I mean I'm not . . ."

"Yes, Ken. You are."

"Are you sure? It's been nearly two months."

"I'm sure, Ken. My periods have never been regular, so I didn't think much about it until recently. I've been tired and a little nauseous in the mornings. Yesterday I went to the clinic, and they confirmed it."

"Lori, I don't know what to say. I can't marry you. I'm only a first year med student. Besides, I'm living with someone else."

"I don't want to marry you."

"Well, what do you want? Money? I could probably send you a couple of hundred for an abortion."

"I don't want anything! I just thought you should know,

that's all!"

"Well, what do you plan to do? You're not going to have the baby, are you?"

"I haven't decided."

"Don't be crazy, Lori! Get it taken care of! It's not a crime. Thousands of women do it every day."

"Good-bye, Ken."

Carmine Pasquale was worried. Jared and Lori had been sitting in that booth together for twenty minutes, and neither one had eaten a thing. He'd taken special pains with the antipasto, and it was just sitting there getting limp. It was a sin to waste food. Especially his food.

Jared and Lori hadn't seen one another since their return from San Diego. Both had agreed that they needed some time apart to sort things out. It had been a long week. Jared could see their differences no closer to resolution, and Lori's dilemma had been multiplied astronomically by the revelation from the clinic.

They sat holding hands across the table. Small talk was the order of the day. The wound was untreatable, so it was ignored while they hoped for a miracle cure. Don't touch. It's too painful. The patient might die right there on the table, next to Carmine's antipasto.

Lori played the game. She talked about school and a one-act play she was rehearsing for. Jared countered with tenant problems and his latest job. All the while, Lori kept thinking to herself.

Lori Klein, what are you going to do? Last week's obstacles were a piece of cake. All you had to do then was forget your career, become a Mormon, get married, and start a family. Hey! You've already started a family. How about that, Taylor? Oh, the other stuff's supposed to come first? You didn't want me to start without you? Picky, picky. Should I tell him? I'm sure the information would do wonders for our relationship.

"Jared, my darling, I have the most wonderful news! I'm going to *have a little one."*

"Are you sure? How fabulous! Are you comfortable, my dearest? Let me get you a pillow. Carmine! A glass of warm milk!"

"What do you think about abortion?" Lori asked Jared.

The question startled him, but his response was immediate. "It's wrong," he said simply.

"Shouldn't a woman have the right to do as she pleases with her own body?" she asked, repeating the popular argument.

"When a woman has an abortion, she's not simply doing something with her body; she's doing something with someone else's body. She causes the life of a completely separate individual to be taken. Feminist rationalization and court decisions aren't going to change that fact. When a woman becomes pregnant, she houses another person for nine months. She has no more right to take that person's life than she does someone's who has already been born. People who come up with that 'It's my body' crap are simply lying to themselves."

"I see," Lori said softly. She didn't try to argue.

"Why do you ask?"

"There's been a flap on campus about it," Lori told him.

"I imagine my view is in the minority."

"Yes."

"I have a hard time discussing that issue without getting angry."

"I noticed."

"Hey, my brother-in-law is back in town."

"Who?"

"Dave Jennings. The director. Remember?"

"Oh. Oh, yes."

"When would you like to meet him?" Jared asked.

"I . . . I don't know. Not right now. I'm under a lot of pressure. I . . . I have to go."

"Lori, listen. I've been climbing the walls this week. I missed you like crazy."

"Please! Please don't!" She grabbed her purse and rose to leave. Jared reached for her arm. She pulled violently away and ran sobbing from the restaurant.

• *THIRTEEN* •

Jared,

I don't believe that we should see one another again. I think a great deal of you, and the past few weeks have been beautiful for me, but there are just too many differences between us. We don't want the same things from life. I wish you all the happiness in the world. I know you'll be successful.

Thank you for a wonderful time.

Lori

Jared read the letter several times. Each time it said the same thing. He threw it in the trash and dialed Lori's apartment. There was no answer. He retrieved the message and read it again. It hadn't changed.

He put on his sweats, drove to the high school track, and began to run. Lap after determined lap he pushed himself around the oval.

Is that it, Klein? Is that all I get? I fall in love with you, give you the best weeks of my life, and all I have to show for it is a crummy half-page letter! "I think a great deal of you. What does that mean? I got better stuff than that in the sixth grade!

Roses are red
Sometimes they're pink,
Jared Taylor,
YOU STINK!
  Sally Sidebottom

Sally had a way with words. You knew where you stood with Sally.

Lots of luck to a real
swell guy. Have fun over
the summer, and I'll see you
next year in high school.
  Love,
  Ruth Ann Hubard

At least I got a 'love' out of Ruth Ann, and she was about as sincere as a Christmas card from your insurance agent.

Dear Jared,
  I'm in Social Studies now, and Mr. Lindop is a really bor-ing teacher. I saw you in the game against Belmont, and you did good. Are you our best player? I think so. I felt terrible when you fouled out. Are you going to the dance Friday? I hope so, and I hope you'll dance with me a lot because I really like you a lot. I always will.
  Love always and forever,
  Carol
  XXXOOOXOXOXOOO
P.S. See you in fifth period Spanish.
P.P.S. Do you like Evelyn Simms? I hope not. UGH! She likes you.

What about that, Lori Klein? I got "Love Always" plus X's and O's from Carol Caruth, and all I ever did for her was buy her a root beer float! Here's a letter for you, Sweetheart!

Lori,

*　　I really love you a lot and hope I always won't. I'll see you in the next life in the telestial kingdom (if I get visitation rights).*

*　　Love,*

*　　Jared*

P.S. Are you going to marry an atheist?

UGH! You deserve each other!

Jared stopped running and lay spread-eagle on the grass, staring at the sky. The anger was spent, the sadness retained. Not even a "good-bye," he thought. When you get the axe from someone you love, they should at least have the courtesy to say good-bye. Maybe this was a different Lori. Maybe the letter was from Lori Hutchinson, the lady with the varicose veins who works in the See's Candy Store. That must be it. Lori Hutchinson. I knew she was crazy about me. Every week when I go in there for my pecan nut roll "fix," she giggles at some marvelously clever thing I say. I wonder what I did to upset her. You'll regret this Mrs. Hutchinson! There are plenty of other candy stores around. You haven't got the only nut roll in the See's!

Good, Taylor, real good. Mrs. Hutchinson would've loved that. Too bad about her.

Jared went home, took a shower, and flopped on the sofa. After a few minutes, he got up and knelt by his bed. He prayed long and earnestly. Lately, Jared's prayers had been brief and shallow. His relationship with the Lord had become casual. During the past ten days, as he wrestled with the reality of the situation between he and Lori, he could hardly bring himself to pray at all. Now the channels were open, and his soul came flooding through. When he finished, he slept.

Rhonda answered the phone, and Jared groaned inwardly. "Hello, Ronda, is Lori there?"

"Who is this?"

"Jared."

"She's not here. She won't talk to you anyway. Don't call back, hypocrite!"

Jared stood listening to the dial tone. *Hypocrite? How did I get to be hypocrite?* he wondered.

Ronda was Lori's roommate, and she was not fond of Jared. She didn't, in fact, like anyone very much. Especially herself. For whatever reasons, Ronda ate too much. Much too much. Jared suspected some of it was caused by her unhappiness by her lack of popularity with the opposite sex, which is the unfortunate lot of most girls who weigh-in over two-eighty. Ronda was also an ardent feminist, and Mormons are not highly regarded by that segment of society.

Nevertheless, Jared thought he had been winning her over. He liked being liked, and it bothered him when someone he knew really didn't like him. Not that he lost any sleep over it. He just thought it was silly and took it as a kind of challenge to make them his friend. Ronda had become a project of his, and he was genuinely friendly to her—asking questions and being interested in her answers. Gradually, Ronda's attitude had changed from hostility, to tolerance, to something bordering friendliness. Thus, he was bewildered by her attack. Hypocrite? What brought that on? "Woe unto ye hypocrites!" He could identify with "woe," but the hypocrite part baffled him.

Jared drove to La Canada where he was remodeling a guest house in the backyard of a wealthy doctor. He worked until past midnight. The doctor and his wife were in Europe, so the noise bothered no one. He tried in vain to lock Lori Klein from his mind.

Maybe I should simply let it go, leave it, he thought. *No, I need to see her again, just to talk for awhile, to say "thank you" and "good luck."* Lori's tearful exit from Pasquales couldn't be the final scene. There had to be a better ending than that.

The phone rang early the next morning, dragging Jared from a fitful sleep. It was Ray Gottier, a contractor and friend.

"Jared, this is Ray."

"Ray, what's up?"

"I need a favor. How busy are you?"

"I'm doing a guest house. Nothing urgent. What do you need?"

"Well, I'm building some condos in Fresno. Rudy got sick, and my mother's having heart surgery tomorrow. I need a foreman for the crew I got up there, or they'll forget the windows. Could you help me out for a few days?"

"I guess so."

"Great. Get a pencil."

Jared arrived back in Los Angeles from Fresno late Saturday afternoon and drove straight to Lori's apartment. A lanky, blonde girl answered the door.

"Ah . . . hello. Is Lori here?"

"Who?"

"Lori. Lori Klein. She lives here."

"Oh, no, she isn't here anymore. She moved out a couple of days ago. I'm Jan," she said, flashing a pleasant smile.

"Moved?! Where?"

"I'm not sure. I guess she went home. Back East somewhere. I know she quit school . . . I had a drama class with her. She told me she was leaving. That's how I got the apartment. I was living in Van Nuys. It really got old commuting from Van Nuys."

"Did she leave a forwarding address?"

"Not with me. You ever been to Van Nuys? Every high school kid in town has a truck or a van. Thousands of 'em."

"Yeah . . . well, maybe that's why they call it Van Nuys."

"Hey! I get it! Van Nuys! That's funny. Van Nuys."

"Say, Jan, I really would like to know where Lori went. If you find out, could you call me at this number?" He gave her a business card.

"Sure," she agreed, "Van Nuys," she repeated, closing the door.

Moved. Why would she move? Did I drive her away? Why would she quit school? It didn't make sense.

Sunday, after church, he called and Ronda answered. Without a word, she promptly slammed down the receiver.

Two weeks later, when the guest house was finished, Jared called his aunt in La Jolla.

"Reet?"

"Hello, Jared."

"I was wondering if I could come down and spend a few days."

"Not right now, Jared. I have company."

"Oh . . . okay. Remember Lori? The girl you met?"

"Of course."

"She quit school and went home."

"I'm sorry, Jared. You're very fond of her, aren't you?"

"Yeah."

"Well, I'm sure things will work out for the best."

"Yeah."

"Call me again soon."

"Okay."

"Jared?"

"Yes?"

"It's going to be all right."

That night, he left for Frazier Park, a small mountain community about seventy-five miles north of Los Angeles. Jared had five pine-covered acres there and was building a cabin to be a vacation spot and writer's retreat.

For the next four weeks Jared worked virtually night and day on the cabin. He came home only on weekends to teach his Sunday School class and take care of any problems with the tenants.

Maynard, the recalcitrant cur, was his only company. Each morning, the two of them would hike in the woods, and then

underway, Jared was in charge of materials, daily planning, and finish work.

He was glad to be busy, but busy as he was he couldn't put Lori out of his mind. Perhaps, he thought, Hawaii had not been a good idea. His proximity to the beach reminded him continually of their first date. Each time he saw the ocean, his memory was invaded by thoughts of a dark-haired girl with a contagious smile and a sinister sense of humor.

• *FIFTEEN* •

Lori pulled the curtain aside and watched as the two young men in dark suits, white shirts, and generic ties dismounted from their bikes and leaned them against a tree in front of the house. Mormon missionaries are hard to miss, she thought. Lori tried to visualize Jared dressed like that, wearing his little black and white badge with "The Church of Jesus Christ of Latter-day Saints" printed beneath his name. *How would I have reacted if he had knocked on my door back then,* she wondered. The thought was a painful one, reminding her of what once was, and what might have been. Would she see him again? Would she be able to face him?

• *SIXTEEN* •

Jared located a branch of the Church a few miles from the worksite in Hawaii, and he was soon comfortable with the warm, gracious people who met there each Sunday. They were the most ethnically diverse group he had ever been associated with. Hawaiian, Chinese, Japanese, Samoan, blacks, and whites all worshipped as one. Jared noted, with only slight disappointment, that there were no eligible girls in the congregation. Marci Chen, the branch president's daughter, was a lovely creature with skin like liquid velvet and eyes like ebony, but she was only sixteen. *Just as well*, he thought, *I'm probably not ready to start anything new right now anyway.*

Shortly after his arrival, the branch held a luau where Jared was encouraged to display his limited musical talents. He did so with some reluctance, because he had known a number of Hawaiians and Samoans in California, and they were all terrific singers and musicians—something in the genes, he concluded. Even so, his contribution was well received and from that time on, Jared was at home there.

The luau was held in a palm-lined patio adjacent to the chapel. During the evening, Jared noticed a sullen young man sitting by himself, leaning back in his chair with his arms folded across his chest. Jared ambled over and took a seat beside the dark, long-haired youth.

"How's it going," Jared asked.

There was no answer, merely a shrug.

"I'm Jared," he said, extending his hand.

The young man took his hand without enthusiasm. Suddenly his interest shifted and he asked, "What did you say your name was?"

"Jared."

"Jared," he repeated, chuckling to himself. "Like in The Book of Mormon?"

"That's the one." Jared conceded.

He laughed again, this time out loud.

"You've got the curse too," he said. "The Mormon curse."

"Mormon curse?" Jared asked.

"Know what my name is?" the boy continued.

"Haven't a clue," Jared confessed.

"Teancum," the young man said. "Isn't that a beauty?"

"Teancum," Jared repeated. "He's one of my favorite Book of Mormon characters."

"My folks too, apparently, but I wish they hadn't stuck me with it. Why couldn't those Book of Mormon guys have names like Bill or Craig or Steve? Then if your parents named you after one of them, it wouldn't be so weird."

"You're embarrassed by your name?" Jared asked.

"Aren't you?" he asked back.

"Not really. Not any more at least. When I was little it used to bother me though."

"I tell people my name is Hank," Teancum explained.

"That's the closest thing I could get out of Teancum. Sounds a little like Teancum, don't you think?"

"Take heart," Jared said. "It could have been worse."

"How?" Teancum wondered.

"Well, our folks might have named us Laman or Lemuel."

The two of them laughed at this small joke that could be appreciated only by a Latter-day Saint.

From the other end of the patio, a white-haired man observed the scene, closed his eyes and silently prayed.

• *SEVENTEEN* •

Jared was sitting at his kitchen table writing a letter the next evening when he heard a knock at his bungalow. Answering the door, he recognized the elderly man whom he had seen at church.

"Brother Taylor," the man said.

"Yes, come in, won't you?"

"I'm Brother Saluone. Tupu Saluone," the man said, extending his hand.

Jared invited the man to sit and asked, "What can I do for you, Brother Saluone?"

"I've come to ask a favor," he said solemnly, "a very great favor." The man's expression and tone signaled that he was gravely serious. "Last night at the luau, I saw you talking with my son," Brother Saluone went on.

Jared thought for a moment. "Teancum?" He asked, thinking that he looked awfully old to be Teancum's father.

The man nodded. "Since moving here from Oahu four months ago, he hasn't been to church. Last night was the first time he's been near the building."

"Feeling a little rebellious, huh?"

"More than a little, Brother Taylor. I'm losing him and I don't know how to get him back. I took that same road when I was his age. I caused a lot of grief for myself and my family.

When I finally got my life back together, I was nearly thirty years old. That's a lot of time wasted."

"Yes it is," Jared agreed.

"A year later, I married Teancum's mother. She was only twenty."

"And you were thirty-one," said Jared.

The man nodded, then continued. "We had six children during the next fifteen years. I worked hard to be a good husband and father. I tried to make up for my past mistakes."

Why is it that a complete stranger is telling me his life history? Jared wondered. And yet, this was not a new experience for Jared. People he barely knew often seemed to feel compelled to tell him intimate details of their personal lives. He had never figured out why.

"Twelve years after our sixth child was born," the man continued, "Teancum joined us. Needless to say, he was a surprise. But he was a beautiful surprise and we loved him very much. Perhaps too much; I know we spoiled him."

"That's not an unusual thing with the youngest child," Jared said, echoing conventional wisdom.

"His mother was forty-six when Teancum was born. We thought her childbearing years were over." The man paused for a moment and gazed out of the window. Haltingly he continued, "Three years ago, Leah died."

"Your wife?" Jared asked.

The man nodded again.

"I'm sorry to hear that," Jared said.

"I didn't handle that very well. I'm afraid I've been a poor father to Teancum since then. Last year he started drinking and hanging around with bums. Then he broke his leg in a motorcycle accident and dropped out of school. The reason I moved here was to get him away from his friends in Kahuku."

Jared wasn't certain where the conversation was leading, but he knew that whatever the man asked of him he would do. Tupu Saluone was a brother in trouble and if he could, he would help because that's what Latter-day Saints do. That's what his father and mother had done, and their parents before them. Once, when his father was a bishop, the family had cut short a vacation in the Sierras to return to Burbank so his father could preside at a funeral and his mother could play the organ.

"But Dad," Jared had complained, "we don't even like these people. Sister Johnson was the biggest gossip in the ward, and her husband isn't even a member of the Church! Why are we doing this?!"

"Duty," his father answered simply.

It was one of the times that Jared resented being a Mormon.

"Be glad we're not Jehovah's Witnesses," offered his older sister, Becky. "They don't even get Christmas presents."

"Shut up," he had mumbled under his breath, just loud enough to receive a warning glare from his mother.

"What's Teancum doing now?" Jared asked, as he returned to the present with an idea.

"Doing? He's not doing anything."

"Is his leg OK?"

"He still limps a little, but it's getting stronger."

"Good."

• *EIGHTEEN* •

"This ain't no government welfare agency we're running here ya know. I'm a businessman," Ray Gottier snapped.

Jared nodded and tried to maintain a solemn expression. He had a bad habit of smiling when someone was acting cantankerous. This rarely improved their mood.

Sitting with Rudy and the Gottiers at their dining room table, Jared had suggested that Ray hire Teancum to work with Jared. The idea had not been well received, and Jared expected that. He knew Ray Gottier. He had been a neighbor and Little League coach. He had also given Jared his first summer job in construction. Jared knew that Ray would ask a few more skeptical questions, then grudgingly agree to "give him a try."

"Does this guy know which end of a hammer to hold?"

"I'll teach him," Jared promised.

"Give the kid a job, Ray," his wife encouraged.

"Give the kid a job, Ray," he repeated, sarcastically. "Can I pay him out of your shopping allowance? If I did he could live like a rock star!"

Everyone sat quietly for a few moments. Rudy, who had stayed out of the discussion, looked up from his crossword puzzle.

"I'll give him a try," Ray said finally.

* * *

Teancum had never liked school. He was mildly dyslexic and scholastic endeavors had always been a struggle. But he was marvelous with his hands. He could make things, improve things, and repair almost anything. With Jared's help, Teancum learned quickly and was soon working independently.

"You got me in trouble with the boss, Hank," Jared informed him one day.

"What'd I do?" Teancum asked, sounding concerned.

"He says you're working out so well that he's thinking about getting rid of me."

"No kidding?!How much do you make?"

"Not what I'm worth," Jared assured him.

"Couldn't live on that, huh?"

"No way," Jared said with a smile.

A doctor had suggested that Teancum ride a bicycle to strengthen his leg, so he and Jared both purchased mountain bikes and began to explore the island together. Work started early, and they were usually through by three, so there was plenty of daylight left to enjoy the scenery. Soon the two of them were taking along sleeping bags and food to spend the night in the mountains or on the beach.

It was a good time for them both. A gentle, genuine bond developed between the blonde California native and his brown-skinned Hawaiian brother. With Teancum's encouragement, Jared bought a baritone ukulele. He couldn't bring himself to get the tiny standard-sized model. It seemed too much like a toy. Each night they would practice together, teaching each other blue grass, Hawaiian, or country western songs.

"Wanna hear something I wrote?" Teancum asked Jared as they sat watching the ocean after sundown one night.

"Sure."

Teancum was silent for a moment. "I never sang this for anyone before."

"I promise I won't laugh."

"It's called 'Wondering.'"

He played a few chords and began a slow, mournful ballad.

Sometimes I wonder why the wind blows.
Sometimes I wonder how a seed grows.
I wonder why we lose those dear
When they're badly needed here.

Wondering if God can hear
Wondering if God can hear

I wonder if He heard me cry
The night my mother said good-bye.
Who was there to wipe my tear
Who was there to calm my fear?

Wondering if God can hear
Wondering if God can hear.

Neither spoke when Teancum finished. Jared wanted to empathize with his friend's pain, unresolved after three years, but he had never lost anyone close. Except for Lori of course, but she wasn't dead. What was he supposed to say—"Nice song"? He said nothing.

"Well?" Teancum said at last.

"He hears," Jared said.

"Why did she die then?"

"I don't know, Hank."

"I thought the Church had an answer for everything."

"No, just some of the big stuff. Why we're here. Where we came from. Our relationship to God and Christ."

Talking long into the night, the two young men exposed their souls in ways that men seldom do. They spoke of faith and family, hopes, and fears. For the first time, Jared talked about Lori. No one had known, except perhaps Rita, how much he cared about Lori.

"How do you know when you're in love?" Hank asked.

"When it happens, you know," Jared shook his head remembering. "Did you have a girl in Oahu?"

"Sort of. Nothing major," Hank answered. Then he asked, "Do you know Marcie Chen?"

"Uh huh."

"My dad says she's cute."

"Haven't you met her?"

"No. She wasn't at the luau."

"Your father's wrong."

"Oh?" Hank sounded disappointed.

"Cute," Jared continued. "Is a term that you use for girls with freckles and a little turned-up nose. Marcie Chen surpasses 'cute' and goes beyond 'pretty'. Miss Chen will short circuit your pacemaker."

"I don't have a pacemaker."

"When you see her, you'll need one."

"Really?"

"Would I lie?"

"Yes."

"You ought to come to church and see for yourself."

"Is this something you and my dad cooked up to get me to church?" he asked suspiciously.

Jared gave him an "Oh brother!" look.

"Why haven't you ever asked me to go to church with you?" Teancum wondered aloud.

"You wanna go to church with me?"

"No."

"That's why I didn't ask."

"Hey, you wanna help me on a moonlighting job?" Jared asked Hank a few weeks later.

"Doing what?"

"Building a deck for one of the members of the branch."

"How much would we make?" Hank wanted to know.
"Probably three or four hundred. I bid it pretty low."
"What's my share?"
"Your share? I thought you'd want to do it for experience."
"Dream on!" Hank countered.
"Well how 'bout a 60-40 arrangement?" Jared proposed.
"Sixty-forty?"
"Yeah. You work sixty hours and I'll give you forty dollars."

• *NINETEEN* •

Following the examination, Lori dressed and joined the doctor in his office as requested. Dr. Selman was a small, tidy man with a high-pitched voice and a deep tan who squinted at you as he talked.

"You're healthy as a horse," the doctor announced to Lori in a congratulatory tone.

"If I break a leg, will they shoot me?" she wondered aloud.

He gave Lori a quizzical look. Doctors are rarely prepared for humor from a patient. "Why . . . no. Of course not," he stammered. Then he decided that the comment had been made in jest and issued a perfunctory smile. "Well," he continued, "you have just over four months left and everything is progressing nicely."

"Good," Lori nodded, without enthusiasm.

"Have you made a decision about the baby?"

Lori could see where the conversation was heading, so she made a detour.

"Yes," she said, "I've decided that I want a girl."

"No. What I meant was . . . what do you plan to do with the baby?"

"I plan to have it," Lori answered.

"Yes, yes, I know that. But, after you have it, what then? I can make arrangements with an agency for the baby to be adopted by a good family."

Lori didn't answer.

"Would you like me to do that?" he persisted.

"No," she answered softly, avoiding his eyes.

The doctor sighed and shook his head. "I hope that you'll reconsider, Miss Klein. Raising a child is difficult under the best circumstances. It's especially hard for a single mother. You won't do the child any favors by keeping it."

Lori silently rose and left the doctor's office.

• *TWENTY* •

Luana Chen answered the door and warmly greeted her visitors. "Jared! Come in." She extended her hand to Hank who appeared unsure whether or not to follow Jared inside.

"Hi Luana. This is Hank Saluone. He works with me."

"Are you Tupu Saluone's boy?" she asked, giving Hank a critical once over.

"Uh huh," said Hank.

"Why haven't I seen you at church?"

"He's waiting 'til he saves enough money for a haircut," Jared explained.

Luana Chen grabbed a handful of Hank's ample mane and proclaimed, "I'll give him a haircut."

"Don't harass the help, Sister C., or you'll never get your deck built," Jared said.

She laughed. "Will you stay for dinner?"

"Sure," said Jared.

"No," replied Hank simultaneously.

Luana peered sternly over her glasses at Hank. "The boss says you stay."

Hank glanced uneasily at Jared.

"He's not the boss," Sister Chen explained with a smile, "I am."

Hank followed Jared through the kitchen and into the back

yard where Jared explained the project. Skater, the Chen's large and stupid golden retriever, loped over and jumped on both of them. Hank wrestled the dog to the ground and engaged him in a game of tug-of-war with an old towel. The scene reminded Jared of Maynard, the wonder cur, whom he had left with a family in Frazier Park. He thought of home and he thought of . . . her. He reflected again on the foolish futility of his involvement with Lori Klein.

How could he have fallen in love with someone so different from himself? What was the attraction? Was it because she seemed so vulnerable to the vagaries of Hollywood . . . a town so corrupted by avarice and ego that villainy is viewed as virtue and integrity rewarded with suspicion or contempt?

Jared searched briefly for an answer before concluding that there was none. Not one at least. It was a package deal. It was the way he felt when he was with her, the sound of her laugh and the peculiar way she cocked her head to one side to appraise him, like a robin searching for a worm. It was the happy way she mocked his singing and his cooking and his dimple, which Jared had on only one cheek.

Hank was so engrossed with Skater he failed to notice that Marcie Chen had joined Jared on the steps by the back door. Jared greeted her, "I brought over a playmate for your dog."

She laughed softly, which attracted Skater's attention and he bounded over to say hello. This left Hank on his back alone in the middle of the yard. Standing awkwardly with an embarrassed semi-smile, he began brushing off his grass-stained clothes.

"Come over here Bowser!" Jared called to Hank. "There's someone you need to meet."

Hank shuffled a few steps closer, locked eyes momentarily with Marcie Chen, then looked quickly away.

"What did I tell you?" Jared said to Hank.

Marcie looked curiously at Jared.

"I was telling my partner here how beautiful you are," Jared explained. This caused Marcie to turn crimson and Hank to peer heavenward as though seeking divine intervention.

"You're awful!" Marcie said as she retreated to the house.

Luana Chen, who had heard the exchange through the kitchen window, cackled in delight.

Later, at dinner, Hank and Marcie avoided looking at one another. Debbie and Darla, ten-year-old twin sisters, pummeled Hank with so many questions that they were finally ordered by their father to remain silent.

Louis Chen was a quiet, reticent man whose ancestors had been brought to Hawaii generations before to work in the fields. His father owned a hotel and a helicopter shuttle service. Louis worked as an agronomist for the state, developing new products that could generate additional revenue for Hawaii and lessen their dependence on tourism.

Luana was a native Hawaiian whose forefathers were there when Captain Cook found the place in 1779. She was warm, outgoing, and outspoken—everything, it seemed, that Louis was not.

Following dinner, everyone retired to the family room where the girls gave a recital for the guests. Marcie played the piano and the twins joined her on the violin and flute.

Hank was clearly stunned by everything about Marcie Chen, a fact that Jared found enormously amusing. While Marcie was accustomed to having boys go goofy in her presence, she still seemed flattered that her charms had had such an affect on Hank.

"Do you think she'd go out with me?" Hank asked Jared as they returned home in the company pick-up.

"Who?" Jared asked, innocently.

Hank shot him a disdainful scowl and chose not to reply. They drove a few more miles in silence.

"She wouldn't," Hank finally concluded, "She's probably a Molly Mormon."

"I suppose," Jared said.

"That stinks!" Hank complained. "Just because she goes to church doesn't make her any better than me."

"Of course not," Jared agreed. "What makes her better than you is that she's beautiful, intelligent, talented, and righteous." Jared paused for a moment, then added, "All the same things that make me better than you."

Jared immediately cracked up laughing, provoking a sharp punch in the shoulder from his friend.

Hank stopped the truck at the bungalow where Jared got out, closed the door, then turned and leaned into the open window. "She likes you, Pard," Jared said. "Don't ask me why, but she does."

On Sunday, for the first time in nearly two years, Hank was in church. He avoided Jared while there, expecting some unwanted sarcasm. Sensing this, Jared gave Hank plenty of space. Hank had no such luck with Luana Chen. She marched up to him after the meeting and announced, "Tomorrow at four p.m.! My house, for a haircut." It was not a request. It was a command, to which Hank gave an apprehensive nod.

Tupu Saluone sought Jared out, grabbed his hand and looked hard into his face. Neither spoke because nothing needed to be said.

• *TWENTY-ONE* •

Persistent pounding echoed through the thin walled bungalow, stirring Jared in his fitful sleep.

He arose and opened the door. It was her. She stood motionless looking into his eyes. She was dressed in white, and beneath the moon's gentle glow, her face was radiant.

"Lori . . . ," he began.

The pounding resumed and Jared shot up in bed and stared blankly about the room.

"Jared!" he heard someone shout. "Hey! Open up!"

"Wait," he called, staggering out of bed and unlatching the door. Ray Gottier stood there, barefoot, wearing a yellow bathrobe with giant red and orange flowers on it.

"What do you want?" Jared groaned, not masking his disappointment that the dream had been just that.

"I came to walk with you in the moonlight!" Ray replied.

"You're dressed for romance," Jared noted wryly.

"Marion bought me this in Honolulu," he said in defense of the bathrobe.

"You're a lucky man, Ray. Your wife doesn't have a younger sister does she?"

"Some woman from California wants you on the phone," Ray grumbled. "Who did you give my number to anyway?"

"Everybody."

"Why don't you get a phone of your own, for cryin' out loud?!"

"Can't afford one," Jared replied, as he slipped quickly into some shorts and a T-shirt. "My boss is too cheap to pay me decent money."

"He's gonna be your ex-boss if he gets any more calls at 1:30 in the morning," Ray threatened. "Don't they know what time it is over here?" Ray grumbled as they made their way to his bungalow.

"You know something Ray?" Jared asked, putting his arm around the shoulder of the small, wiry man that he worked for.

"What?"

"You're beautiful when you're angry."

• TWENTY-TWO •

Lori rose awkwardly and shuffled to the bedroom window. She lifted it slightly to allow some fresh air to blow in and returned to bed. Lying on her back in the darkness, she placed both hands on her swollen stomach, feeling the movement of the tiny person inside.

"Hi there," she said softly. "Ready to come out and see the world? It's kinda scary out here. I hope you don't make as many stupid mistakes as your mother. Do you want to stick with me and try to make a go of it? Some people think I should give you away. That would be really hard. I'd do it though, if I believed it was best for you—if I couldn't properly care for you. But I've talked to God about it . . . and I think . . . I think maybe we should stay together. That okay with you?"

She had spoken often with her unborn baby about the future. Lori's parents had agreed that she could keep the child and return to live with them. They had a large house and plenty of money, and while they were not happy about the circumstances of her pregnancy, they were pleased at the prospect of being grandparents for the first time. While living with her parents, Lori could return to school. The bright lights of Hollywood had lost their appeal. She had decided to work instead toward a degree in special education, which now seemed much more meaningful.

• *TWENTY-THREE* •

The two men sat quietly in the airport lounge waiting for the departure announcement. When it came, both stood slowly and shook hands. Then they seized one another in a quick, rough embrace.

"I'll miss you, Pard," Jared said.

Hank only nodded, hoping not to betray his emotion.

"I'll come back and speak at your missionary farewell," Jared continued.

"Might take ya' up on that," Hank replied.

"Good. Well . . . take care." Jared slapped Hank on the shoulder, then turned and headed down the ramp to the plane.

Although the phone call from Margaret Morales had not been good news (a fire had destroyed two units in his apartment building and damaged a third), he felt a certain sense of relief for the excuse to return to California. For several weeks, he had been strangely restless, feeling that he should be elsewhere, doing other things, but he had no notion of where or what.

Before going to Hawaii, he had turned his father's real estate holdings over to a property management company, and though they had done an adequate job, he felt the need to assume responsibility again. Also, he was lonely. Jared hadn't been on a real date since he and Lori had parted ways.

Hank and Jared had been cajoled into squiring a couple of female Easter week vacationers from Iowa about the island for a few days, but other than that, his social life had been nil. *That's going to change when I get home,* he thought to himself.

• *TWENTY-FOUR* •

It was okay being back at Pasquales. Jared liked the way the place smelled and the casually disheveled atmosphere. He hadn't intended to come here, but a business matter had brought him to the area so he decided to stop by. Pasquale's brought memories of Lori, but on this day the memories felt good. He savored them as he did the meatball sandwich with bell peppers and Monterey Jack cheese.

Halfway through his sandwich, the door opened and in waddled Ronda the Rotund and three friends. She didn't notice Jared until she was opposite his booth, a few feet away. Suddenly she froze and regarded him contemptuously, her nostrils flaring like a nervous colt. "It's him!" she shrieked.

Jared offered a wan smile and nodded slightly, "Wonderful to see you again, Ronda."

"He's the one! The one I told you about!" The fat finger of fate was flailing in his face. "My roommate's friend! The girl from New York."

"OH! HIM!" they exclaimed in near unison.

I'm famous, Jared thought.

"The hypocrite!" Ronda added for further clarification. Naturally.

"Pig! Chauvinist pig!" contributed another, getting into the spirit of the occasion.

Now we're getting to the good stuff.

"Just look at him, sitting there!"

I'm supposed to stand for insults?

"Disgusting," offered a stringy-haired girl.

"We ought to scratch his eyes out!" volunteered another, who looked like she was up to the job.

Oh, oh, the mood's getting ugly.

"Look, Ronda, I don't know what . . ."

"Don't play dumb with me. I know everything! You get Lori pregnant, then you refuse to marry her because she's not a Mormon. But you won't let her have an abortion. Oh, no, that would be sinful!"

"What?"

"So she has to leave school! She has to endure months of suffering! And you sit here free as a bird!"

"Lori's pregnant?" Jared asked incredulously. "She told you?"

"I have a friend at the clinic who told me. So the secret's out!" Ronda crowed triumphantly.

It was impossible. How could she . . . ? he thought. *She did talk to me about abortion. . . . No, Ronda's crazy. . . . that was the last time I saw her. Could she have been . . . ?*

The picture would focus, blur, then come in sharply again. Jared worked frantically with his mental dials, trying to get the images right. Ronda and the Rondettes meanwhile continued their verbal assault in quadraphonic sound. After several confused moments, Jared rose slowly to his feet.

"Ronda," he said deliberately, his voice choking with emotion, "You've got the wrong guy."

In five giant strides, he arrived at the entry of the restaurant and swung the door open. Carmine Pasquale shouted to him as he left, "Jared, you better marry that girl."

Jared got into his car and drove aimlessly. All the pain and emotion of the past months came flooding back, magnified tenfold. The memories he had tried to bury suddenly resurrected themselves and crowded into his mind.

They were walking hand in hand on the beach. They were making tostadas in his kitchen. They were standing by the piano in the Magic Castle, singing.

That had been a memorable evening. The room was full of noisy, laughing people, but as Lori sang, the place grew quiet, and people from adjoining rooms came to listen. After each number, the applause and audience grew until virtually the whole club was crowded in and around where Lori was singing. Jared just stood there with a kind of proud, happy grin. Afterward, a man in a fur coat with black, shoulder length hair approached Lori and introduced himself. He said he was a record producer and wondered if she was under contract with anyone. Jared stepped forward and put his arm around Lori's shoulders. The two men exchanged cool greetings.

"Hello, Jared," the man said.

"Lenny," Jared nodded slightly.

"Oh, you two know each other," Lori gushed.

"Mr. King is in the record business, Jared."

"That's interesting. Since when?" Jared asked.

"Well, I'm not actually in the record industry myself. But I have some very heavy contacts who are."

"I'm sure you do," Jared said. "The young lady's interested in a film career, Lenny. Maybe you could steal a good script for her."

Lori suddenly sensed the tension in the air and glanced nervously at Jared, then at the long-haired man. Lenny King's smile had been replaced by an ugly, twisted sneer.

"Get lost, Worm," Jared said.

There was a hard edge in Jared's voice, something Lori had never heard before. The man opened his mouth as if to argue then reconsidered, smiled thinly and walked away.

"What was that about?" Lori asked.

"Lenny King is a guy who makes his living stealing material from unknown writers and comics. He stole a script outline from a friend of mine and sold it for seven thousand dollars."

"How does he do that?"

"Pretends to be your friend, offers to help you with your stuff. Get it to the right people. He has 'heavy contacts' in the industry."

"Sounds like a swell guy. I wonder what he wanted from me?"

Jared gave her a skeptical look and shook his head. "Lori, my love, I don't think you're quite ready for Hollywood."

That was the night Jared knew. He knew for the first time that he wanted to be with Lori Klein always. Be with her and protect her from the Lenny Kings of the world.

The reality of the present came flooding back into his senses. Had she been living a lie? Had she been seeing someone else all along? No. Jared knew that wasn't possible. Whatever had happened between her and someone else had happened before they met. But it had happened. Could he deal with that? He didn't know. He did know that he had to see her.

He drove to UCLA and tried to get her home address from the admissions office. Sorry, that information is confidential.

Next he called a friend who works for the LAPD.

"Detective Mendoza speaking."

"Felix. This is Jared. I need some help."

"Hey, stranger, where have you been keeping yourself?"

"I've been working in Hawaii."

"Soft touch. What can I do for you?"

"I need to locate a girl who was a student at UCLA. She left school several months ago. Lives in New York on Long Island. I wonder if you could get her home address from the school?"

"What for?"

"Well, it's kind of personal, Felix. She's a close friend, and I need to find out where she is."

"That's all you're going to tell me? You know what you're asking me to do is illegal, don't you?"

"If it were legal, I wouldn't need your help, you pompous turkey. Call it an investigation. She stole something from me."

"What?"

"My heart. It was pure gold."

"Oh, brother. Hold on while I get my violin."

"Felix, this is really important. I've got to find her."

"What's her name?" he asked, noting the urgency in Jared's plea.

Ten minutes later, Jared had the address.

• *TWENTY-FIVE* •

Hello, Mom. I'm in love.
That's good.
She's Jewish, Mom.
That's bad.
She's pregnant, Mom.
That's worse.
But I'm not the father. Mom? You still there?

The 747 landed at Kennedy Airport a little after six a.m. Jared shaved and put on a fresh shirt in a restroom at the terminal. Then he rented a car and headed for Bay Shore on Long Island.

Listen, Dad, I've got some good news and some bad news. First, I want you to know that I'm in love with a pregnant Jew.
What's the good news?
I just told you.
What's the bad news?
I just told you.

What's going to happen when I do see her, Jared wondered. *It's probably stupid for me to come here. Maybe she won't even talk to me.*

* * *

Mom, I've got good news and bad news. The good news is I'm in love with this Jewish girl, and she's going to have a baby.
. . . Let's save the bad news for another time, Son.

What will I say? Where do we go from here? What's changed?

When Jared arrived in Bay Shore, he stopped at a mini market, bought a pint of orange juice, and took a nervous walk. When he regained his courage, he got back in the car and drove to the home of Benjamin Klein.

Dad, I want you to know that I'm in love with this terrific girl, but I'm not about to be a father.
That's fine, Son.
But this terrific girl that I'm in love with is Jewish, and she's about to become a mother.
Who is this?

The house was a huge multi-level job, surrounded by a tall, wrought iron fence. The gate was locked. He pushed a button and waited.

"Yes?" came a voice over the speaker, which was concealed in a well-manicured shrub.

"Ah . . . I'm Jared Taylor, and I've come to see Lori."

There was a pause that seemed like a year to Jared.

"Come in, Mr. Taylor."

The electronic gate swung open, and he drove up the long, circular driveway. A small, dark-haired woman came out to greet him. It was evident where Lori got her good looks.

"I'm Ruth Klein," she said, extending her hand, along with a warm smile.

"Hello," Jared shook her hand.

She led him inside to a large, open living room where he was invited to sit down.

"Have you had breakfast, Mr. Taylor?"

"Yes. Well . . . no, but I'm not hungry right now, thanks."

"How was your trip? Did you fly in this morning?"

"Yes, yes I did. The trip was fine, Mrs. Klein."

"Ruth. Please call me Ruth."

"Mrs. Ruth . . . er . . . Ruth . . . I would like to see Lori."

"I'm sure that you would, but she's not here."

"Well, do you mind if I wait?"

"I'm afraid you've come a long way unnecessarily, Jared. Lori's in California."

"California?"

"She's staying with your aunt in La Jolla. Her father and I were out there several months ago when she joined your church."

"She what?"

"Am I going too fast for you?" she smiled. "Lori was baptized into your church."

"Mrs. Klein, I'm really sorry. I had no idea . . ."

"Why are you sorry?" she laughed.

"Well, I'm sure you feel bad about her leaving . . ."

"Lori left Judaism years ago. She seems content with her new faith. She's going to meetings and singing in the choir. She has a lovely voice, you know."

"Yes, I know."

"Her father appears to be delighted. Ben thinks most religion is bunk, but he has great respect for the Mormon people. We're happy for her." She was quiet for a moment, then she said, "Jared, I'm afraid I have some very bad news for you."

His body stiffened.

"Lori's expecting a baby. Any day now," she added.

Jared closed his eyes and breathed an audible sigh. "I know that, Mrs. Klein. That's why I'm here."

"How did you find out?"

"I ran into her old roommate yesterday. She accused me of being the father, among other things, said she had a friend at the clinic who told her of the pregnancy."

"I see."

"Mrs. Klein, uh, Ruth, did Lori say anything to you about me?"

"Oh, yes, a great deal."

"Well, what did she say? About me? I mean, how does she feel?"

"I think she's very much in love with you."

"Why didn't she tell me that? Why did she run away?"

"Jared, Lori is carrying another man's child. That's very difficult for her to cope with. She feels guilty, and unworthy of you. I should think you would have difficulty with that too."

He sat without speaking for a time. "Do you know the . . . fellow?" Jared couldn't bring himself to say "father."

"Yes. His name is Kenneth Green. We know his family. They live in Bellport. He's a medical student. He and Lori dated most of the summer before she left for UCLA. Toward the end of the summer he succeeded in convincing her that virginity is out of style, and they became intimate."

Neither spoke for several moments. As he sat staring at the floor, Jared noticed a flying ant with one wing askew, limping determinedly across the deep-pile carpet. Insects have incredible will, he thought. Probably no feelings, just blind will. Maybe people would be happier that way.

The silence was finally broken by Lori's mother. "What are your plans now, Jared?"

"I'm in love with your daughter, Mrs. Klein. I'm going to marry her."

"And what about the child?"

"I . . . I guess that's up to Lori."

He rose to leave. "I guess I'll see you at our wedding."

Mrs. Klein's face showed mild astonishment. "Hadn't you better check with my daughter first?"

"Let's surprise her."

She laughed. "Lori told me you have a marvelous sense of humor."

"It's been in hibernation for awhile. Maybe I can break it out for our next visit."

"I'm sure you will, Jared. You're a remarkable young man."

"I'll take good care of your daughter, Ruth."

"Thank you. Thank you very much."

• *TWENTY-SIX* •

Rita Lundgren was setting the table for dinner when the doorbell rang. It rang twice more in the brief time it took her to walk to the front door. "Hold your horses, for heaven's sake," she mumbled. It was Jared. She was expecting him.

"You know why I'm here?"

"Yes. Lori's mother called."

"Where is she?"

"On the beach, walking."

"Does she know I'm coming?"

"Yes."

"You should've told me, Reet."

"I couldn't. I promised."

He turned to go.

"Jared," Rita called.

He stopped and looked back.

"She's frightened."

"That makes two of us," he said.

Lori's back was to him when he first saw her. She was wearing baggy sweat pants and the oversized shirt that he had given her on their first date. She walked slowly along the firm, wet sand at the water's edge, her sandals dangling from one hand.

He ran after her. Lori turned when she heard the footsteps.

Jared slowed and stopped a few yards away. They stood, looking at each other.

"Here I am," she said finally, "barefoot and pregnant."

Jared rushed to her and held her close. They stood clinging to one another for a long time. Softly her tears began to flow.

"It's okay," he said. "It's okay now."

"Why did you come?" she asked at last.

The question bewildered him.

"I look awful," she complained. "I've never looked so awful."

"Is this a permanent condition?" Jared asked.

"Shut up," she said through her tears.

"Do you want me to leave?"

"Yes."

"I won't."

"Good."

Jared held Lori gently as she continued to cry and he pondered the curious nature of the woman he loved. "Will you marry me?" he asked, after what he considered an appropriate pause for courtship.

She shook her head without looking up. "I can't," she sobbed.

Jared thought on that for a moment.

"Can't?" he asked.

"I'm not good enough for you."

"I know," he agreed. "But you're the one I love, so I guess I'm stuck with you."

She looked at him now. "Don't mock me Jared," she pleaded.

He gave her a sad, apologetic smile.

"I'm not like you," Lori went on. "I don't care about obnoxious teenagers or old men running around in their underwear."

"Lori, don't . . ."

"Let me finish," she insisted, putting one hand to his lips. "I've decided to keep this baby. She's my responsibility, but I couldn't ask you to share that responsibility."

"It's a girl?" Jared asked.

Lori nodded.

"How do you know?"

"From a sonogram the doctor did."

"I'm glad it's a girl. I hope she looks like you."

"Jared, are you listening to me?"

"Uh huh."

"We're not going to get married. I can't go to the temple with you."

Now it was Jared's turn to be serious. He took her tear streaked face in his large hands and looked hard into her eyes. "Listen to me," he said in a tone both gentle and firm. "The day of your baptism you walked out of that water as pure as a new baby. What happened before we met is history. The Lord has forgiven you. That's what repentance and baptism is all about. Now you have to forgive yourself."

"What about you, Jared? Can you forgive me? Can you live with . . . this?" She put her hand on her stomach.

"I'm here, Lori," he said. "That's why I'm here."

She turned from him now and walked slowly up the beach. He fell into step beside her, put one arm around her shoulder and offered a tissue with his free hand. She accepted the Kleenex, gave it a robust blast, and stuck it in the pouch of her sweatshirt.

"It wouldn't be right," she persisted. "We're no good for each other."

Jared declined comment. It was, he realized, a futile time for debate. As the two walked wordlessly along the shore, Lori put an arm around Jared's waist and leaned her head on his chest. Suddenly she stopped and turned to him with a startled expression. "I think you'd better take me to the hospital."

• TWENTY-SEVEN •

"You're the husband?" the admitting nurse asked, looking up from her form.

"Well . . . no, I'm her fiance," Jared replied.

"No he's not," Lori corrected from her wheelchair across the desk.

"He's not your fiance?" the nurse asked Lori.

"No."

"Yes, I am," Jared insisted.

The nurse, a grey-haired woman with a businesslike air, now returned her attention to Jared. "Young man," she said archly, "I believe if this woman were engaged to you, she would be aware of it."

"She's forgetful," Jared said.

"I am not," said Lori.

"I presume then," the nurse continued, "that you're the father."

"That's right," Jared affirmed.

"He is not!" Lori protested.

The nurse looked at Lori, then back to Jared.

"I'm not the biological father," he admitted.

"There's another kind?" the woman asked dryly.

"Yes. The real kind. The kind that walks the floor with a baby when they have colic, the kind that helps with homework and drives kids to soccer practice. The kind that runs down the street hanging onto the seat of a bicycle when they're learning to ride. The kind that prays at their bedside when they're sick . . . the kind who's *there*."

The woman was silent for a moment. Then she looked at Lori. "Who is this man?" she asked.

"My fiance," Lori replied in a voice choked by emotion.

• *TWENTY-EIGHT* •

Jessica Elizabeth was almost seven months old when her mother joined hands with Jared across an altar in the Washington, D.C., Temple, and they were married for "time and eternity." Some who witnessed the ceremony claimed that angels were in attendance. When asked about the rumor, Jared replied only, "Mine was."

• ABOUT THE AUTHOR •

Gary Davis was born in Provo, Utah, and raised in Southern California. He is a former comedian and newspaper columnist. His writing has also appeared in *The New Era* and *The Reader's Digest*. "I'm hopeful that I'll make enough from sales of this book to get a nose job and still have money left over for a haircut at Bill Clinton's Beverly Hills barber," Gary claims.

Gary studied English at Brigham Young University where he had a "singularly undistinguished academic career." He is, however, a very funny man, and critics rave about his dialogue and style. Gary and his wife Jean have four children and reside in Frazier Park, California. This is his second novel.